Adrian blinked back the sudden sting of tears.

Gideon would have loved to see Faith's animals, and Lovina would have liked this new neighbor with her ready smile and determined ways. It was so unfair that their lives had been cut short. So unfair that he had to go on living without them.

He heard Faith softly inquire, "What's wrong?"

He took the pan from her. "My wife and son passed away not long ago."

"I'm so sorry. You must miss them very much."

"I do."

Adrian met Faith's gaze. Oddly, he found he wanted to talk to her about Lovina and Gideon.

He hadn't been able to save his wife or his son. That bitter truth haunted him day and night.

He blinked hard to clear his vision. Faith's face swam into view. She understood. He saw it in her eyes. It was more than sympathy and compassion. She had been in the same dark place that surrounded him.

Books by Patricia Davids

Love Inspired

His Bundle of Love
Love Thine Enemy
Prodigal Daughter
The Color of Courage
Military Daddy
A Matter of the Heart
A Military Match
A Family for Thanksgiving
*Katie's Redemption
*The Doctor's Blessing
*An Amish Christmas
*The Farmer Next Door

Love Inspired Suspense

A Cloud of Suspicion
Speed Trap

*Brides of Amish Country

PATRICIA DAVIDS

After thirty-five years as a nurse, Pat has hung up her stethoscope to become a full-time writer. She enjoys spending her new free time visiting her grandchildren, doing some long-overdue yard work and traveling to research her story locations. She resides with her husband in Wichita, Kansas. Pat always enjoys hearing from her readers. You can visit her on the web at www.patriciadavids.com.

The Farmer Next Door

Patricia Davids

Love Inspired

LOVE INSPIRED BOOKS

ISBN-13: 978-0-373-87679-2

THE FARMER NEXT DOOR

And all the women that were wise hearted did spin with their hands, and brought that which they had spun, both of blue, and of purple, and of scarlet, and of fine linen.
—*Exodus* 35:25

This book is dedicated
with deep love and affection to my mother, Joan,
a true wise hearted woman.

Chapter One

If the Amish farmer standing outside her screen door would smile, he'd be a nice-looking fellow—but he certainly wasn't smiling at the moment. His fierce scowl was a sharp reminder of all her life had been before—tense, fearful, pain-filled.

Faith Martin thrust aside her somber memories. She would not allow the past to follow her here. She had nothing to fear in this new community.

Still, the man at her door made an imposing figure blocking out much of the late afternoon sunlight streaming in behind him. His flat-topped straw hat sat squarely above his furrowed brow. That frown put a deep crease between his intelligent hazel eyes.

Above his reddish-brown beard, his full lips barely moved when he spoke. "*Goot* day, *Frau*. I am Adrian Lapp. I own the farm to the south."

His beard told her he was married. Amish men were clean-shaven until after they took a wife. He had his pale blue shirt-sleeves rolled up exposing brawny, darkly tanned forearms folded tightly across his gray vest. A familiar, nauseous odor emanated from his clothes.

Faith's heart sank. It was clear he'd had a run-in with one of her herd. What had he been doing with her animals?

She managed a polite nod. Common courtesy dictated she welcome him to her home. "I'm pleased to meet you, neighbor. I am Faith Martin. Do come in."

He made no move to enter. "Is your husband about?"

It seemed the farmer next door wasn't exactly the friendly sort. That was too bad. She had prayed it would be different here. "My husband passed away two years ago. It's just me. How may I help you?"

Her widowed status seemed to surprise him. "You're living here alone?"

"Ja." She brushed at the dust and cobwebs on her apron and tried to look like a woman who managed well by herself instead of one who'd bitten off far more than she could chew.

His scowl deepened. "Your creatures are loose in my fields. They are eating my beans."

Faith cringed inwardly. This was not the first impression she wanted to make in her new community. "I'm so sorry. I don't know how they could have gotten out."

"I tried to catch one of them by its halter, but it spat on me and ran off with the others into the cornfield."

She saw the green, speckled stain across the front shoulder of his shirt and vest. Alpaca spit, a combination of grass and digestive juices, was unpleasant but not harmful. What a shame this had to be her new neighbor's first introduction to her alpacas. They were normally docile, friendly animals.

Faith never tired of seeing their bright, inquisitive faces waiting for her each morning. Their sweet, gentle natures had helped her heal in both body and spirit over the past two years.

"The one wearing a halter is Myrtle. She's the expectant mother in the herd. You must have frightened her. They are leery of strangers."

"So I noticed," he answered drily.

"Spitting is their least endearing habit, but it will brush off when it dries." Faith's encouraging tone didn't lighten his scowl. Perhaps now wasn't the time to mention the smell would linger for a few days.

"What did you call them?"

"Alpacas. They're like llamas but they have very soft fleece, softer than any sheep. Originally, they come from South America. How many did you say were in your field?"

"I counted ten."

"Oh, no!" Fear blotted out any concern for her neighbor's shirt. If all of her animals were loose in unfamiliar country, it would be difficult, even impossible, to round them up before dark.

Her defenseless alpacas couldn't spend the night out in the open. Stray dogs or coyotes could easily bring down one of her half-grown crias, or they might wander onto the highway and be hit by a passing car. She couldn't afford the loss of even one animal. She had everything invested in this venture and much more than money riding on her success.

Please, Lord, let me recover them all safe and sound.

As much as she hated to be seen using her crutch, Faith grabbed it from behind the door. It was wrong to be vain about her handicap, but she couldn't help it. It was a personal battle she had yet to win.

The pickup truck that had crashed into their buggy two years ago had killed her husband and left her with a badly mangled leg. Doctors told her it would be a miracle if she ever walked again, but God had shown her mercy. After a long, difficult recovery she was able to get around with only her leg brace most of the time. But chasing down a herd of frisky alpacas required exertion and speed. Things she couldn't manage without added support.

She pushed open the screen door, forcing Adrian Lapp to

take a step back. She didn't miss the way his eyes widened at the sight of her infirmity.

Let him stare. It wasn't something she could keep secret. She knew her crippled leg made her ugly and awkward, a person to be pitied, but she wouldn't let it be her weakness. Right now, the safety of her animals was the important thing, not her new neighbor's opinion of her. "Where did you see them last?"

"Disappearing into the cornfield beyond the orchard at the back of your property."

"I will need to get their halters and lead ropes from the barn." She left him standing on the porch as she made her way down the steps.

Adrian quickly caught up with her. "I'm sorry, I didn't know... I will take care of the animals for you. There is no need for you to go traipsing after them."

His offer was grudgingly given, but she sensed he meant well.

"I'm perfectly capable of catching them." She didn't want pity, and she wasn't about to leave her valuable livestock in the hands of a man who didn't even know what kind of animal they were.

Hobbling ahead of him across the weedy yard, she spoke over her shoulder. "Once I catch them, can you help me lead them home?"

"Of course."

Faith headed toward the small, dilapidated barn nestled between overgrown cedars some fifty yards from the house. In the harsh August sunlight it was easy to see the peeling paint, missing shingles and broken windowpanes on the building. The Amish were known for their neat and well-tended farmsteads. She had a lot of work ahead of her to get this place in shape.

She didn't know why her husband had never mentioned

owning this property in Ohio or why he had chosen to leave it sitting vacant all these years, but finding out a month ago that she owned it couldn't have come at a better time.

She pulled open the barn door. Copper, her mare, whinnied a greeting. Faith spoke a few soft words to her as she gathered together the halters and lead ropes that were hanging on pegs inside the doorway.

Adrian took them from her without a word and slipped them over his shoulder. She was grateful for his help but wished he wasn't so dour about it. Why couldn't her alpacas have chosen to eat the beans of a cheerful neighbor? Maybe she didn't have any.

She led the way around the side of the barn to the pens at the rear. The gate panel that should have been wired closed had been pushed over, offering the curious alpacas an easy way out. Why hadn't she paid more attention when her hired help set up the portable pen and unloaded the animals? Now look what her carelessness had wrought.

Adrian removed the thin wire that had proven to be an ineffective deterrent. "Do you have a heavier gauge wire than this or some strong rope?"

"I'm sure there's something in the barn that will work."

"Then I should find it." He turned back toward the barn door.

Faith called after him. "Shouldn't we find my animals first and then worry about how to keep them in? It's getting late."

He didn't even glance in her direction. "It won't do any good to bring them back if they can just get out again."

She pressed her lips closed on a retort. She had learned the hard way not to argue with a man. Her husband had made sure she understood her opinions were not valued.

Leaving her new neighbor to rummage in the barn, Faith headed toward the rows of trees that stretched for a quarter of a mile to the back edge of her property, knowing he could easily overtake her. It was slow going through the thick grass, but at least she knew her alpacas would be well-fed through the summer and fall once she had her fences in place.

It didn't take long for Adrian to catch up with her. As she expected, his long legs made short work of the distance she had struggled to cover. A twinge of resentment rippled through her before she firmly reminded herself it didn't matter if someone could walk faster than she could. All that mattered was that she walk upon the path the Lord had chosen for her without complaint.

Adrian wasn't sure what to make of the woman charging ahead of him through the tangled grass of the old orchard. Her handicap clearly didn't slow her down much. He'd been curious about his new neighbors as soon as he'd spotted the moving van and large horse trailer inching up the rutted lane yesterday.

The farmstead had been deserted since he'd been a lad. It hurt his soul to see the good farm ground lying fallow and the peach orchard's fruit going to waste year after year. He could do so much with it if only he had the chance.

Even though he'd seen he had new neighbors, he hadn't gone to introduce himself. He didn't like meeting people or answering questions about his life. He liked being alone. He preferred to stay on his farm and work until he was bone-tired and weary enough to fall asleep as soon as his head hit the pillow at night.

Too tired even for dreams…or for nightmares.

He wouldn't be here today if Faith Martin had kept her animals penned up properly. This was costing him an afternoon of work that couldn't wait.

He glanced sideways at her. She was a tiny slip of a woman. She didn't look as if she could wrest this land and buildings back into shape by herself. A stiff wind could blow her away. Why, the top of her head barely reached his chin whiskers.

A white prayer *kapp* covering her chestnut-brown hair proclaimed her to be a member of the Plain faith, but he didn't recognize the pattern. Where had she come from?

She wore a long blue dress with a black apron and the same type of dark stockings and sturdy shoes that all the women in his family wore. As she walked beside him, the breeze fluttered the long ribbons of her *kapp* about her heart-shaped face, drawing his attention to the slope of her jaw and the slender curve of her neck. She was a pretty little thing with eyes bright blue as a robin's egg. She had long eyelashes and full pink lips.

Lips made for a man to kiss.

He tore his gaze away as heat rushed to his face. He had no business thinking such thoughts about a woman he barely knew. What was wrong with him? He'd not taken this much notice of a woman since his teenage years.

He used to look at Lovina that way, used to imagine what it would be like to kiss her. When they wed he discovered her kisses were even sweeter than he'd dreamed. After her death, he'd buried his heart with her and raised their son alone until…

So what was it about Faith Martin that stirred this sudden interest? He studied her covertly. She pressed her lips into a tight line as she concentrated on her footing. Did walking cause her pain?

Her eyes darted to his face, but she quickly looked away as if she were uncomfortable in his presence. Her glance held a wary edge that surprised him. Was she frightened of him?

He hadn't meant to scare her. He quickly grew ashamed for having done so. He wasn't used to interacting with new people. Everyone in his family and the community knew of his desire to live alone. He truly had no reason to be surly with this woman. Her alpacas hadn't actually damaged his crop.

He glanced at her again. How could he set this right? How could he bring back her smile?

Adrian abruptly refocused his attention to the task at hand. He had a corncrib to finish and more work waiting for him at home. He didn't have time to worry about making a stranger smile. He would help her gather her animals and then get back to his labors. A few moments later they reached the end of the orchard.

The fence that separated her land from his had fallen down long ago. Only a few rotting uprights remained to mark the boundary. Beyond it, his cornfield stood in tall, straight rows. There was no sign of her odd creatures. They could be any-where by now.

Faith cupped her hands around her mouth and called out, "Myrtle, Candy, Baby Face. Supper time."

He listened for any sound in return but heard only the rustle of the wind moving through the cornstalks. What did an alpaca sound like? Did they moo or bleat?

She took a step farther into the field. "Come, Socks. Come, Bandit."

Suddenly, a wooly white face appeared at the end of the row a few yards away. He heard Faith's sigh of relief.

"There's my good girl. Come, Socks." The animal emerged from the corn and began walking toward her with its head held high, alert but wary. It was butternut-brown in color with a white face and four white legs. Its head was covered with a thick pelt of fleece, but the long neck and body had been recently shorn, leaving the animal with an oddly naked ap-pearance. It approached to within ten feet, but wouldn't come closer.

Faith glanced at Adrian. "Give me one of the halters and a lead rope and wait here."

He had no intention of venturing closer. Although the animal looked harmless, he still reeked of Myrtle's earlier disapproval.

Faith walked toward Socks with her hand out. The animal made a low humming sound, then ambled up to her and wrapped its long neck around her in a hug.

"Were you lost and scared? It's okay now. I know the way home." She crooned to it like a child as she slipped the halter on, then scratched behind the alpaca's ear.

A second animal stepped out of the corn. It already wore a halter. Adrian recognized it as the one that had spit on him. As soon as she caught sight of him, she turned back into the cornfield.

Faith led Socks to Adrian and handed him the lead rope. "Try not to scare her. If one gives an alarm cry, they may all scatter."

Faith took several halters and ropes from him and disappeared into his cornfield without another word. Adrian found himself alone with the strangest animal he'd ever beheld.

He studied the creature's face. It was calmly studying him in return with large, liquid black eyes fringed with long black lashes. Besides doe-like eyes, Socks had a delicate muzzle with two protruding lower teeth. Her narrow, perked ears reminded him of a rabbit. Her round body was similar to a sheep, but she had long legs like a deer. Looking down, he saw two large, hooked toenails on each front foot that could have belonged to a giant bird.

When Socks tried to nibble his beard, he drew back abruptly, uncertain of her intentions. "I have orders not to scare you."

Socks hummed softly and didn't spit.

So far, so good.

Reaching out, Adrian scratched behind her ear as he'd seen Faith do. Socks closed her eyes and nuzzled into his hand. Her thick wool was as soft as anything he'd ever touched. He smiled at the sound of her hum. They might be odd-looking creatures, but they had a certain appeal. When they weren't spitting.

He ran a hand down her camel-like neck. She stood, patient and unconcerned. With his confidence in her temperament restored, he gave free rein to his curiosity. He wanted a closer look at her strange feet.

As soon as he grasped her leg, Socks lifted her foot as any well-trained horse would do. To his surprise, the bottoms of her feet were soft pads much like a dog's foot, not a hoof at all.

Straightening, he stroked her nose and chuckled. "It appears the Lord assembled you from leftover animal parts."

Socks looked past him and called softly. He turned and saw another alpaca, this one black as night, emerge and look in his direction. Should he call out to Faith or would that scare the animal?

It looked more curious than frightened. He gave a gentle tug on the lead rope and walked with Socks toward her friend. He made a soft humming sound, hoping to soothe the animal and not frighten it into running away. Was he going to help Faith, or was he about to make things worse?

Tired, hot and discouraged, Faith emerged from the forest of corn thirty minutes later with only two of her alpacas in tow. The sun was touching the horizon. It would be dark within the hour. How would she find the others then? She would need dozens of people to comb this acreage properly in the dark.

It seemed she was destined to meet more of her neighbors tonight and not under the best of circumstances.

She had no doubt they would come to help. That was the Amish way. She would not be prideful. She would ask Adrian Lapp to gather a group to help in her search.

To her surprise, Adrian wasn't where she had left him. She glanced around, wondering if she had come out of the corn in the wrong place. No, this was the spot. Had he gone back to his own work? What kind of neighbor was he, anyway?

"I shouldn't be judgmental. Perhaps his work is as pressing as mine." As usual, Myrtle proved to be a good listener and followed obediently behind Faith.

"All I have to do is round up my missing animals, start a business and ready a dilapidated house to pass inspection in a week's time so I may become the guardian of my brother's child. I'm sure Mr. Lapp is equally as busy."

Tears pricked the backs of Faith's eyes as she struggled through the long grass. The past two years had been incredibly hard. First, there had been the terrible crash and her husband's death. She'd spent weeks in the hospital afterwards. Her small savings had covered only a fraction of her medical bills. Thankfully, the congregation at her church had taken up a collection to pay the rest, but it left her little to live on. It had taken her more than a year to get back on solid financial ground.

Then, three months ago came word that her brother and his wife had been killed in a flash flood, leaving their five-year-old son an orphan. As the boy's only relative, she was willing and eager to take Kyle in. She'd been halfway through the maze of paperwork and home studies needed to approve his adoption when her landlord had informed her he had to sell the farm she'd been renting.

Her adoption plans fell apart. She couldn't take in a child when she was about to lose the roof over her head.

But in the midst of her despair, the Lord had delivered what seemed like a miracle. A delinquent property tax statement had arrived in the mail addressed to her husband. It was then that she'd learned she owned a house and farm in Ohio. She'd spent every penny she could scrape together to pay the bill and move.

She hadn't expected to find the place in such deplorable condition.

Was this God's way of telling her Kyle didn't belong with her? Did He want Isaac's child raised in the English world her brother had chosen instead of in her Amish faith?

Why would God see fit to give Isaac's child into her care when He had denied her children of her own?

She had no answers to the questions and doubts that plagued her. It would be all too easy to sit down and bawl like a baby, but what would that fix? She sniffed back her tears and blinked hard, refusing to let them fall.

Tears hadn't made her husband a kind man. They wouldn't bring back her brother or undo any of the pain she had endured. They certainly wouldn't build fences for her alpacas, clean her house or make it a home for a lonely little boy.

She stopped to rest her aching leg and looked heavenward. "I know You never give us more than we can bear, but I could use Your strength right now. Help me, Lord. I beseech You."

As always, she felt the comfort of God's presence in her life whenever she turned to Him. She must not let her despair or her fears gain the upper hand. God was watching over her.

Had not the letter come in her hour of need telling her she owned this land? So what if it was going to take hard work to make it livable? She knew how to work. God would provide. She had faith in His mercy. Here in Ohio she had started Kyle's adoption process again. Now she had to prove to a new agency worker that she had a safe home and a stable income.

Which was exactly what she didn't have yet.

Drawing a deep breath, she started forward again. The time for tears was past. This was the new path the Lord had chosen for her. She had to believe it would be better than the life she'd left behind.

Chapter Two

When Faith emerged from the trees, she stopped short in surprise. Adrian Lapp stood beside her barn with all eight of her missing alpacas clustered around him in their pen. It seemed her prayers had been answered, and apparently her grumpy neighbor had a way with animals.

Not two minutes ago she had been piling unkind thoughts on his head.

Forgive me, Lord. I judged this man unfairly. I won't do it again.

Walking up to Adrian, she said, "I can't believe it. You found them."

"It was more like they found me."

Bandit stood close beside him, sniffing at his beard. He gently pushed the inquisitive black alpaca away and opened the gate so Faith could add her two to the herd. Adrian said, "I fixed the pen. They shouldn't get out again."

"Thank you. I was so worried I wouldn't be able to find them before dark. This move has been hard on all of them."

"And on you?"

Her gaze locked with his. Did she look like such a mess? She must. Embarrassment sent heat flooding to her face. Socks chose that moment to nibble at the rim of Adrian's straw hat. He pushed the alpaca gently aside. Faith concentrated on removing the halters from her pair.

"Where have you come from, Faith Martin? Surely not South America like your animals."

His interest seemed genuine. Some of her discomfort faded. "Originally, I'm from Indiana, but on this move I came from Missouri."

"That's a lot of miles."

It was, and many more than he knew. Her husband had been affected with a wanderlust that had taken them to twelve different communities in the ten years they'd been married. Faith was determined that this farm would be her final home. She wanted to put down roots, to become a true member of a community, things she'd never been able to do during her marriage.

Besides, she had to make a home for Kyle. A place where her brother's child could recover from the tragedy of losing his parents and grow into manhood. This was her last move. If it was God's will, she didn't plan to leave Hope Springs, Ohio until He called her home.

"I'm grateful for your help, neighbor. I have fresh lemonade in the house. Can I offer you a glass?"

He opened the gate and slipped out, securing the panels with a quick twist of heavy wire, then double checking it to make sure it would hold. "*Nee.* I must get back to my work."

With her overture of friendship soundly rejected, she nodded and started toward the house.

He hesitated, then fell into step beside her. "What are your plans for this place?"

Oddly pleased by his interest, she said, "I want to enclose the orchard area with new fence. In the future I will divide it into separate pens so I can rotate where the alpacas graze. In spite of their behavior today, the fencing is really to keep predators out. My babies won't try to wander once they become accustomed to their new home. After that, I need to fix up the barn well enough to store winter hay for them." She walked slowly, more tired than she cared to admit.

"So my beans will be safe in the future?"

He hadn't really been interested in her plans, only in making sure his crops wouldn't be destroyed.

"*Ja,* as soon as I have the fences up. Of course, I will pay for any damages my animals caused."

"That won't be necessary. Do you plan to do all this work yourself?"

Faith paused and drew herself to her full height of five-foot-one. "I'm stronger than I look. I'm not afraid of hard work. With God's help I shall manage."

His eyes grew troubled. "I was going to offer the names of some young men who could use the work. That is why I asked. I did not mean to offend."

He had a gruff manner, but he was clearly sorry to have upset her.

Her defiance drained away, leaving her embarrassed. "I don't have the money to pay a hired man. Once I sell the yarns I am spinning, I will consider hiring someone."

"A light purse is nothing to be ashamed of."

"You're right, but I don't want people here to think I will be a burden on them."

"We would not think such a thing, Faith Martin. It would be un-Christian." There was a hint of rebuke in his words.

Amish families and communities supported all Amish widows and orphans. It was everyone's responsibility to care for them, but Faith needed to be able to take care of herself.

At her age and with her disability, she had no hope of marrying again. Even if such an offer came her way, she would never place her fate in the hands of another man. No, never again. The thought of doing so sent cold chills down her spine.

She looked up to see Adrian studying her intently. His frown had returned, but she wasn't frightened by it now. It was more bluff than substance.

He said, "If you find this farm is more than you can handle, I'll be happy to take it off your hands. For a fair price."

"I'm not interested in selling. I plan on staying here a long, long time."

"Then I pray you fare well among us, but do not forget my offer."

Faith watched as he strode away with long, easy strides. She saw a man at ease in his surroundings and at home on his own well-tended land. Not overly friendly, but not unfriendly. She found him…interesting. If his spouse was pleasant, they might prove to be good neighbors. She liked the idea of having someone close by to count on in an emergency.

She had turned down his offer to buy the place, but she sensed he didn't believe she could make a go of it on her own.

Why shouldn't he doubt her? She doubted herself. For years Mose had hammered into her head what a failure she was as a wife. She couldn't give him children. It was her fault all his business enterprises failed because she didn't work hard enough.

In her heart she knew he was wrong, but after a while it ceased to matter. She had simply accepted the unkind things he'd said and kept quiet.

But Mose was gone now, and she had to believe in herself again. This was the time and place to start.

Watching Adrian cross the field toward his farm, she wondered what it would be like to have a strong, handsome man like Adrian Lapp for a husband? She shook her head at her foolish musing.

A woman could not tell if a man would be a good husband by his looks. Mose had been a handsome fellow, but his good-looking face had hidden a mean nature at odds with the teachings of their Amish faith.

She forgave Mose for the good of her own soul. He was standing now before a just God, answering for his sins while she was free to live a quiet and humble life. It would be enough.

She wondered if other Amish wives suffered silently as she had done. She prayed it wasn't true. In her heart she wanted to believe in the gentle nature of men who professed submission to God in every aspect of their lives—but there was no way to be certain. Only God could see into the hearts of men.

Pushing aside the host of unhappy memories gathered during her marriage, Faith entered her new home determined to finish sweeping away years of debris and clutter, from the house and from her heart. She was ready for her new beginning.

"I heard someone has moved into the old Delker place. Do you know anything about it?" Ben Lapp handed the next set of boards up to Adrian who was perched on the top of the new corncrib.

Adrian knew there would be no end to his brother's curiosity. He might as well tell him everything he knew. "*Ja,* I met her yesterday. Her name is Faith Martin. She is Amish and a widow."

"I don't suppose she has a pretty daughter or two?" Ben asked hopefully. At seventeen, Adrian's youngest brother was in the first year of his *rumspringa,* his running around time, and always on the lookout for new girls to impress.

Adrian hated to dash his hopes. "Sorry, but she said she was alone."

"Too bad. A pretty new face would be welcome in this area."

Adrian recalled Faith's soft blue eyes and the sweet curve of her lips. "She is pretty enough."

"Really?"

Adrian caught the sudden interest in Ben's tone and grinned. "Pretty enough for a woman in her thirties."

Ben's face fell. "She's an old woman, then."

"Do you consider me old? I'm but thirty-two."

Adrian tried not to smile as he watched the struggle taking place behind his baby brother's eyes. Finally, Ben said, "You're not so old."

"Not *so* old. That's good to know for I was thinking of getting a cane when I went to market."

The thought of a cane brought a sudden vision of Faith struggling through the long grass with her crutch. How was she doing today? And why was he thinking about her again?

Ben grinned. "Tell me more about the widow. What's she like?"

Determined, pretty, kind to her animals, wary, worried. A number of ways to describe his new neighbor darted through Adrian's mind, but they all sounded personal, as if he'd taken an interest in her. "She raises alpacas."

"Alpacas? Why?"

"She spins their fleece into yarn for sale."

"I remember grandmother Lapp sitting at her spinning wheel. It was fascinating to watch her nimble fingers at work even when she was very old."

"I remember that, too."

"I never understood how chunks of wool became strands of yarn. Whatever became of her spinning wheel?"

"I suppose it's in *Mamm*'s attic if one of our sisters doesn't have it."

"It's sad to think someone is living at the Delker farm now."

"Why do you say that?" Adrian hammered the last board in place.

"Because we could eat all the peaches we wanted from those trees. No one cared. Now, we'll have to get permission. Is the house still in decent shape?"

"From the outside it doesn't look too bad. I'm not sure about the inside." Maybe he should stop in again and see if there was something Faith needed done around the place. That would be neighborly.

Not that he was looking for an excuse to see her again. He wasn't. He grew annoyed that she kept intruding into his carefully ordered world.

Ben backed down the ladder. "Do you even remember the people who lived there before?"

Adrian followed him. "I remember an old *Englisch* woman yelling at our cousin Sarah and I when we were helping ourselves to some low-hanging fruit. I must have been ten. She scared the daylights out of us. I think she went to a nursing home not long after that. When she passed away, the place stayed vacant."

"Is the new owner a relative?"

"That I don't know."

"Didn't you try to buy the place a few years ago?"

"More than once. I got a name and address from the County Recorder's office and sent several letters over the years, but no one ever answered me. I even tried to buy it from her yesterday, but she wasn't interested in selling." He could still hear the determination in her voice when she turned him down.

Determination was one thing. A strong back was another. She'd need both to get that place in working order.

"It's odd that she'd show up after all this time. I wonder why?" Ben mused.

Gathering together his tools, Adrian started toward the house. He'd spent more than enough time thinking about Faith Martin. "It's none of our business."

"Not our business? Ha! Tell that to *Mamm*. She'll be wanting every little detail, and she'll have it by Sunday next or I'll eat my hat." Ben fell into step beside Adrian.

It irked Adrian that he couldn't get Faith off his mind. What was she doing? Were her alpacas safe? Was she having trouble putting up fences for them? It would be a big job for one woman alone.

Ben wrinkled his nose in disgust. "What's that smell?"

Adrian swiped at the shoulder of his vest. The dried juice had brushed off, but not the aroma. "Alpaca spit."

"That's nasty. I didn't know they spit."

"Only if you scare them."

"I'll avoid doing that."

"Me, too, from now on."

"Before I forget, *Mamm* wanted me to remind you to come to supper tomorrow night."

Alerted by the sudden uncomfortable tone in Ben's voice, Adrian stopped. "Why would I need reminding? I come to supper every Wednesday evening with the family."

"That's what I told her."

Adrian closed his eyes and sighed deeply. "Who is it this time?"

"Who is what?" Ben looked the picture of innocence. Adrian wasn't fooled.

Leveling a no-nonsense, tell-me-the-truth look at his brother, Adrian repeated himself. "Who is it this time?"

"Edna Hershberger," Ben admitted and flinched.

"Edna? She's at least fifteen years older than I am."

"Her cousin is visiting from Apple Creek. Her younger female cousin. I hear she's nice-looking."

"Why does mother keep doing this?" Adrian started walking again. He wasn't interested in meeting marriageable women. He would never marry again. He had sworn that over his young wife's grave when he'd laid their son to rest beside her.

"Mother wants to see you happy."

"I am happy." The moment he said the words he knew they were a lie.

"No, you're not. You haven't been happy since Lovina and Gideon died."

The mention of his wife and son sent a sharp stab of pain through Adrian's chest. He bore wounds that would not heal. No one understood that. "I'd rather not talk about them."

"It's been three years since Gideon died, Adrian. It's been eight years since Lovina passed away."

"For me, it was yesterday."

God had taken away the people he loved, leaving Adrian an empty shell of a man. An empty shell could not love anyone, certainly not God, for He had stripped away the most important parts of Adrian's life.

Adrian went through the motions of his faith, but each day it became harder to repeat the platitudes that no longer held meaning for him. Disowning his Amish faith would only lead to being separated from his remaining family. For their sakes he kept his opinions about God to himself.

Ben laid a hand on Adrian's shoulder. "You can't blame *Mamm* for worrying about you."

Adrian met his brother's gaze. "Mother needs to accept that I won't marry again. You can tell her I've made other plans for tomorrow evening."

"What plans?" Ben called after him.

Adrian didn't answer him. Instead, he walked to the end

of his lane and up the road for a quarter of a mile to where a small field of tombstones lay enclosed by a white wooden fence. A fence he painted each year to keep it looking nice.

He opened the gate and crossed the field to where an old cedar tree had been cut down. The stump made a perfect seat for him to sit and visit with his wife and son.

The breeze blew softly across the open field. Beyond the fence he saw fat black-and-white cattle grazing in a neighbor's pasture. Overhead the blue sky held a few white clouds that changed shape as they traveled on the wind. He took off his hat and looked down at the small tombstones that bore the names of his wife and child.

"It's another pretty day, isn't it, Lovina? I remember how much you enjoyed the summer evenings when the days stretch out so long. I miss sitting with you on the porch and watching the sun go down. I miss everything about both of you."

Tears filled his eyes as emotions clogged his throat. It took a minute before he could go on.

Clearing his throat, he said, "We've got a new neighbor. Her name is Faith Martin. I think you'd like her. You should see the strange animals she has. They spit. I think I like sheep better and you know how much I dislike them."

Clasping his hands together, he leaned forward with his elbows propped on his knees. "*Mamm* is at it again. She's trying to fix me up with a cousin of Edna Hershberger. I wish she would learn to leave well enough alone. I don't want anyone else. You will be my only wife in this life and in the next. If Gideon had lived, it might have been different."

The tears came back, forcing him to lift his head. "A boy needs a mother, but he's with you now. I know that makes you happy because it gives me comfort, too."

He sniffed once and wiped his eyes with the heels of his hands. "I'm not going over to *Mamm*'s for supper tomorrow. I'm sorry if that disappoints you. I've decided to go over to

Faith Martin's. That place needs too much work for a woman alone to do it all. I can spare an hour or two in the morning and again at night. The days are long now," he added with a wry smile.

The memory of Faith declaring she wasn't afraid of work slipped into his mind. "She reminds me of you a little bit in the way her chin comes up when she's riled. She said an odd thing yesterday. She said she didn't want people here to think she would be a burden. It makes me wonder who made her feel that way in her last community."

Having said what he needed to say, he rose to his feet. "Enough about our neighbor. Give Gideon a kiss for me. I miss you, Lovey."

So much so it was hard to put into words. "Sometimes, I wake at night and I still reach for you. But you aren't there and it hurts all over again."

As he walked away, he wondered if Faith Martin woke in the night and reached for the husband who was gone.

Chapter Three

Faith woke to the sound of a persistent clanking coming from outside her house. Squinting, she could just make out the hands of the clock on her dresser. Six thirty-five.

Her eyes popped open wide. Six thirty-five! Panic sent her heart racing. Mose would be so angry when he discovered she'd slept late.

Throwing back the sheet, she sat up and stopped as every muscle in her body protested the quick movement. Had he beaten her again? What had she done wrong this time? She couldn't remember.

Swinging her feet off the mattress, she reached for her clothes. They weren't on a chair beside the bed. Looking around the strange room, she saw them hanging from a peg on the wall. Her panic dropped away like a stone from her chest. She drew a deep breath.

Mose might be gone, but his imprint remained in her life. In moments of mindless panic like this one. In nightmares that left her weak and shaking in the night.

Faith began to recite her morning prayers, letting the grace of God's presence wash away her fears and restore her peace.

Dear Lord, I give You thanks for this new day, for my new

*home and for the strength to face whatever may come my
way. I know You are with me, always. Watch over Kyle and
keep him safe. If it is Your will, Lord, let him join me here,
soon. Amen.*

A few years ago her morning prayers had been much simpler. *Please don't let me make Mose angry today.* Sometimes,
she wondered if she would ever be truly free of him.

She stood and crossed to the open window. The sound of
hammering started up again. It was coming from her orchard,
but she couldn't see anyone. What was going on?

She dressed and set to work quickly brushing out her hip-
length hair. When it was smooth, she parted it straight down
the middle and began to make a tight roll of it along her hair-
line pulling all of it together and finally twisting the remain-
der into a tight bun, which she pinned at the back of her head.
With her hair secure, she donned her *kapp* and pinned it in
place. Outside, the clanking continued.

Sitting on the edge of the bed, she buckled on her leg
brace, wincing as the padded bands came into contact with
her chafed skin. She was paying for all the time she'd spent
working and sweating the past few days. She needed to apply
more salve to the reddened areas, but that would have to wait.
Her priority was finding out what was going on outside.

After leaving the house, she limped to the barn to check on
her animals. Copper dozed in her stall. The alpacas, all ten of
them, as Faith quickly counted, stood or lay in their pen outside. Relieved, but with mounting curiosity, Faith made her
way into the orchard.

A few yards from where she had stopped building fence
the evening before, Adrian Lapp was pounding a steel fence
post into the ground. He'd already added several stakes along
the string she had laid out to mark the boundary of her pen.

What was he doing here? She hadn't asked for his help.
As quickly as her objections surfaced, she swallowed them.

Humility was the cornerstone of her Amish faith. Being humble also meant accepting help when help was offered.

Adrian hadn't seen her yet. She watched as he effortlessly drove in the stakes with a metal sleeve that fit over the top of each post. Compared to the heavy maul she had used to painstakingly pound each post into the ground, his tool made the job much easier. And he didn't even have to stand on the wooden box she had used just to reach the top of the six-foot-tall t-posts.

All right, he was strong and tall. It was a great combination when building fences, but that didn't mean she needed to stand here staring. She had half a mind to go back to the house and let him finish the row, but her conscience wouldn't let her. This was her property now. She was the one who needed to take care of it.

"Guder mariye," she called out in her native Pennsylvania Dutch, the German dialect spoken by the Amish. "You've done a lot of work while I was lazing abed. *Danki.*"

He stopped pounding, wiped the sweat from his brow with his shirtsleeve, and nodded in her direction. "Good morning to you, too. You have accomplished quite a bit here yourself."

His gaze swept across the posts that she'd put in yesterday, the yard she had mown into order with an old scythe and the fresh laundry waving on the clothesline she'd strung between two trees beside the house.

"I could have done more if I'd had a fence post driver such as you have there." She walked toward him to look at the tool.

"They aren't expensive. You can pick them up pretty cheap at farm auctions."

"I will keep that in mind."

It seemed to Faith that he wanted to say more, but instead,

he returned to pounding the post he was working on until he'd sunk it another two feet into the ground.

"I appreciate your help, Mr. Lapp, but I can manage on my own. I'm sure you have plenty of work to attend to."

"Call me Adrian. I've got a few free hours today. Do you have a wire stretcher? I can put up the fencing after I get these posts in if you do."

"It's in the barn along with the rolls of woven fence wire I want to use. Are you sure you have time to do this? I hate to impose."

"I'll do the posts this morning and come back this evening to finish putting up the wire. Unless you object?" He grabbed another stake, measured off the distance with a few quick steps and began hammering the post into the ground.

"That will be fine." Other than taking care of her animals, she would have the whole day free to work on the house. Adrian's help was a blessing she hadn't anticipated.

Still, she had plenty to do to get the house ready for the social worker's arrival next Wednesday. Would God understand if she did a little extra work on Sunday? Sundays were days of rest and prayer and a time for visiting with friends and family even if there wasn't a service.

Since Amish church services were held every other Sunday, she would have another week before she had to face the entire congregation. Would they all be as kind and helpful as her new neighbor? He had a gruff way about him, but his actions spoke loudly of a kind heart.

After watching Adrian work for a few more minutes, Faith realized there was nothing she could do to help him and she was wasting time. She left him to his work and returned to the house giving thanks to God for her neighbor's timely intervention.

Inside the house she applied salve to her chafed leg, then set about making breakfast and a pot of strong coffee. An hour later, just as she was pulling a pair of cinnamon coffee cakes from the oven, Adrian came to the screen door.

She fought back a smile. With the windows wide open to the morning breeze, she had been sure the smell of her baking would reach him.

He said, "I finished the row of posts you had laid out."

She set the second hot pan on the stovetop. "Already? You've saved me a lot of work. *Danki.* Would you like some coffee?"

He hesitated, then said, "I would."

When he came inside, her kitchen instantly felt small and crowded. Unease skittered over her skin. She moved away to make more room between them.

He looked for a peg to hang his hat on, but there wasn't one. He settled for tossing it on the sideboard and took a seat at her table. When he wasn't looming over her, Faith could breathe better.

He motioned toward the wallpaper with its faded yellow flowers. "You will have a lot to do to make this a plain house."

"*Ja.* It will be a big task. Every room is wallpapered." She tapped the floor with her foot. "This black-and-white linoleum will be fine but there is pink-and-white linoleum in the bathroom."

The colorful flooring and wallpaper would all have to be taken out. The Amish lived in simplicity, as they believed was God's will. They avoided loud colors and worldly things such as electricity in order to live separate from the world. Hopefully, the bishop in her new community would give her plenty of time to make over the house from English to Amish.

She would have the option of painting her walls blue, green or gray. The brightly patterned linoleum on the bathroom floor would have to go. She could leave the planks underneath bare or replace the linoleum with a simpler, more modest color. It was all on her list of things to be done. A list she was whittling down much too slowly.

She cut two pieces of coffee cake and carried one of them along with a cup of coffee to the table. Adrian accepted her offering with a nod of thanks. "The county will take down the electric lines leading to the house, but you will have to take down the ones leading to the barn."

"I know. At least the gas stove still works and I was able to have the propane tank filled before I arrived."

Fetching a cup of coffee and a piece of cake for herself, she said, "I've cooked on a wood-burning stove, but I'm not a good hand at it."

Adrian's look of sympathy said it all. She sat down at the table with a heavy sigh. "I take it the *Ordnung* of this church district doesn't allow propane cook stoves?"

"*Nee,* we do not. The stove must be wood-burning or coal-burning. But you may have a propane-powered refrigerator and washing machine."

The thought of chopping wood or hauling coal on top of her other chores was enough to dampen her spirits. She glanced sadly at the stove. It was old, but it worked well. She would hate to see it go.

It was always this way when she moved to a new community. Each Amish church district had their own rules about what they allowed and what they didn't. Each bishop in charge of a district often interpreted those rules differently.

She had lived in several communities that used tractors in the fields instead of horses. When they'd lived in Mifflin County, Pennsylvania, their church district permitted members to drive only yellow buggies, another place only gray ones. Here in Hope Springs the buggies were black.

She would have to make all new *kapps* for herself, too. The women of each district wore distinctive patterns. She would get around to that if, and only if, she met with the approval of this community and they voted to accept her as a new church member.

If they didn't accept her, she would have to look for another nearby district who would or live as an outsider. "I must meet with your bishop soon."

"Bishop Zook is a good man. He will help you learn your way among us."

"Is he a good preacher?" she asked, half in jest. Church services often lasted three or more hours.

"I've only fallen asleep twice during his sermons." Adrian didn't crack a smile, but she saw the twinkle of humor in his eyes. It surprised and delighted her.

"Then he must be *wunderbarr.* I'm looking forward to my first church Sunday already."

Adrian changed the subject. "Are you a relative of Mrs. Delker, the woman who used to own this place?"

"No, but Mose, my husband, was a grandchild of hers. I inherited this farm after he passed away. It's odd really, because he never once mentioned owning a farm in Ohio."

"I tried to buy it from him about five years ago."

"Did you? That must have been when we were raising chickens in Nebraska. Why did he say he wouldn't sell?"

They had certainly needed the money. The chicken houses had been another of her husband's failed business ventures. They'd left Nebraska owing money to everyone from the feed store to their landlord. Only Mose's last venture, buying her first four alpacas, had actually turned out well.

She never understood how her husband talked people into loaning him money for his wild ideas or how he could just pick up and walk away without looking back or even feeling badly for those who'd lost money because of him. Every time they moved, they left hard feelings behind.

Would this new community receive her into the church if they knew her husband had left debts unpaid all across the

Midwest? She was sorry now that she had mentioned Nebraska to Adrian.

"Your husband didn't give a reason why he wouldn't sell. He never answered my letters."

She wanted to tell Adrian how lucky he was *not* to have done business with her husband, but she wouldn't speak ill of the dead. She rose and took her cup to the sink. "We moved around a lot. Perhaps your letters missed him."

"Perhaps. Do you find it hard to talk about him?" he asked quietly.

"Yes." She kept her back to Adrian. It was hard to talk about Mose because there was so little she could say about him that was good.

"I understand."

The odd quality in his tone made her look at him closely. The pain in his eyes touched her heart. Why was he so sad?

He rose abruptly and crossed the room to pick up his hat. "I must be going."

"Wait a moment." She quickly wrapped the remaining coffee cake in a length of cheesecloth and added a small package wrapped in brown paper and string to the top. She held it out to him. He stared at her as if he didn't understand.

"It's a small token of my appreciation for all your hard work. A pair of socks made from my alpaca yarn. Please tell your wife that she is welcome to visit anytime. I'm sure she and your children will enjoy meeting my animals."

Adrian blinked back the sudden sting of tears. Gideon would have loved to have seen Faith's animals and Lovina would have liked this new neighbor with her determined ways. It was so unfair that their lives had been cut short. So unfair that he had to go on living without them.

"Is something wrong?" Faith inquired softly.

He took the packages from her. "My wife and son passed away."

"I'm so sorry. You must miss them very much."

Adrian met Faith's sympathetic gaze. Oddly, he found he wanted to talk about Lovina and Gideon. Somehow, he knew Faith would understand.

"I miss them every day. My son would have liked your alpacas. He had a way with animals, that boy did. He was always finding lost and hurt creatures and bringing them home for me to make well."

"Little boys believe their fathers can do anything."

"Too bad it isn't true."

He hadn't been able to save his wife or his son. That bitter truth haunted him day and night.

He blinked hard to clear his vision. Faith's face swam into view. She understood. He saw it in her eyes. It was more than sympathy and compassion. She had been in the same dark place that surrounded him.

"How old was your son when he died?" she asked.

"Four."

"You mustn't think me cruel, but four years is a gift. I wish I might have had four years, even four days, with my daughters."

"You've lost children, too?"

"Twin daughters who were stillborn. I always wondered if that was why Mose was never able to settle in one place. If we'd had a family, maybe things would have been different. Only God knows."

"I wanted at least six children. Lovina wanted a dozen or more. Gideon was the first and he was perfect."

Adrian couldn't believe he was talking to this woman about his family. He hadn't been able to talk to anyone about them since Gideon's death. Maybe it was because she'd known the same kind of tragedy that he felt she understood what he was going through. Maybe it was because Ben had brought the subject up yesterday.

Whatever the reason, Adrian suddenly decided not to bare more of his soul. Remembering was too painful.

He said, "The coffee cake is appreciated. I'll be back tonight to help finish your fence. I need my bean crop kept safe from your overgrown rabbits."

"Your help has been most welcome, neighbor."

He settled his hat on his head and walked outside into the summer sunshine. At the foot of her steps, he stopped and looked back. She stood framed in the doorway, her arms crossed, a faraway expression in her eyes. He wondered what she was thinking about.

Was she thinking about the children and husband she had lost or the work that needed to be done? Did she find it hard to go forward with her life? Somehow, he didn't think so.

Faith Martin was a remarkable woman.

The moment the thought occurred to him, he began walking, putting as much distance as he could between himself and his disturbing neighbor.

He'd come to Faith's home today to do his Christian duty by helping a neighbor, but he'd also been interested in seeing exactly what shape the place was in. The more he saw, the less he expected she would be able to manage it alone.

He might yet be able to buy the land. If he made some improvements for her, well, that would mean less work for him later.

Having a fence around the orchard was a good idea. Letting the alpacas graze down the overgrown grass would make it easier to mow later, or he could put sheep in to do the same job.

At the edge of his hay meadow, he stopped and glanced toward Faith's house once more. Helping her might turn out to be a good idea—from a business point of view. Not because he wanted to spend time in her company.

His wife might be gone, but he wouldn't be untrue to her. Lovina had been the one love of his life. He had no business thinking about spending time with another woman.

He had come to Faith's place to lend a hand. He hadn't been looking for sympathy or a shoulder to cry on. He hadn't planned on finding someone who could understand the pain he lived with. Yet, that was exactly what he'd found with Faith Martin.

Was that why he found her so attractive? His feelings toward her troubled and confused him.

He had already promised to help her. He wouldn't go back on his word. As promised, he would help her get her home in order as a good neighbor should, but he wouldn't spend any more time alone with her.

Chapter Four

It was shortly before noon on Saturday when Faith heard the sound of a horse and buggy approaching the house. She dropped the sponge she'd been using to wash grimy windows into her pail, dried her hands on her apron and waited to see who had come calling.

The buggy stopped in front of her gate, and three Amish women stepped out. They all carried large baskets over their arms.

"Guder mariye," called the oldest woman. She wore a bright, beaming smile of welcome. Behind her came a young woman with black hair and dark eyes followed by another woman with blond hair.

"Guder mariye," Faith replied. A faint flicker of happiness sparked inside of her. She was free to make new friends here—if they would have her. She wouldn't have to hide her bruised face or bear pitying looks from those who suspected her husband's cruelty.

The leader of the group stopped at the bottom of Faith's steps, adjusted her round wire spectacles on the bridge of her nose and switched her heavy basket to her other arm. "Welcome to Hope Springs. I am Nettie Sutter."

She indicated the dark-haired girl standing behind her. "This is my daughter-in-law, Katie."

"And I am Sarah Wyse," the blonde added. "My cousin is your neighbor to the south."

"Adrian?"

Sarah nodded. "When I heard he'd met you, I thought it best to rush over and assure you the rest of Hope Springs is more hospitable than Adrian is."

"He has been most kind and welcoming."

"He has?" Sarah exchanged astonished glances with her companions.

Faith swept a hand toward the front door. "Do come in, but please excuse the condition of the house."

"None of us can keep our houses free of dust in the summertime. With all the windows open to catch any breeze, the dust piles up before you know it."

Faith had more than a sprinkling of dust to contend with. She had twenty years worth of accumulation to haul out. She was thankful that she had made a coffee cake for herself while making one for Adrian that morning. At least she had something to offer her guests.

The women gathered around the kitchen table, each one setting her basket on it. Sarah opened the lid of the one she carried and began to pull out its contents. "We brought a few things to help you settle in and get this old house in order."

Out of her basket, Sarah brought cleaning supplies, plastic pails, pine cleaner, rags, sponges and brushes. "Where shall we start?"

Faith was speechless. She hadn't expected help from the community so soon.

Nettie picked up the pail and carried it to the sink. "I will finish these windows for you. Sarah, why don't you take a broom to the front porch and steps? Elam, Eli and his boys will be here to paint this evening."

"I'll get this food put away." Katie opened her basket and brought out two loaves of bread and a rhubarb pie with a gorgeous lattice crust just begging to be eaten. A second later she began unpacking mason jars filled with canned fruits and vegetables.

Faith was overwhelmed by their kindness. "*Danki*. This is far too much."

"No thanks are needed," Nettie assured her.

Perhaps not needed but gratefully given. Faith asked, "Who are Elam and Eli?"

Nettie smiled broadly. "Elam is my son and Katie's husband. Eli and his sons live down the road a piece. Our farm is a little ways beyond that toward Hope Springs."

"Where do you need me to start?" Katie asked, looking over the kitchen.

Faith took a second to gather her thoughts. "I've cleaned out one bedroom upstairs, but the others haven't been touched in years. If you want to start in one of them, that would be great. Sarah, perhaps you could help me drag the mattresses outside so I can beat the dust out of them."

Sarah held out her hand. "Lead the way."

The house quickly became a beehive of activity. Old bedding was taken out, walls and floors were scrubbed free of grime and rubbish was hauled out to the burn barrel. Everywhere inside the house, the crisp scent of pine cleaner filled the air. In one afternoon the women managed to do more inside the house than Faith had accomplished in four days on her own.

Her heirloom clock was striking five when the women gathered in the kitchen once more. Faith wiped her forehead with the back of her sleeve. "I don't know about you, but I've worked up an appetite. I believe I will sample this pie. Would anyone else care for a piece?"

Nettie smiled brightly. "I thought you'd never ask."

"Where are your plates?" Sarah was already moving toward the cabinets.

"To the left of the sink." Chuckling, Faith turned to Katie. "Would you like some?"

"Yes! I could eat the whole thing."

Nettie grinned. "That's because you are eating for two."

Faith endured a sharp stab of wistfulness but quickly recovered. "Congratulations. When is your baby due?"

"The last week of November."

"Is this your first?" Faith gathered forks for everyone and brought them to the table.

Katie shook her head. "It will be my second. We already have a little girl, so we're hoping for a boy."

Nettie sliced into the pie and slipped a piece onto the plate Sarah supplied. "Either will be fine with me as long as it is a healthy grandbaby."

Faith decided it was the perfect opening to share something about herself. "I am expecting a little boy soon."

Everyone's glances fell to her trim waist. She chuckled as she appeased their unspoken curiosity. "I'm hoping my nephew can come to live with me soon. That's why I have to get this house in some kind of order."

"Is he visiting for the summer?" Sarah asked. The women all took a seat at the table.

Sadness put a catch in Faith's voice. "*Nee,* he is not coming for a visit. I hope he will live with me until he is old enough to marry and have a family of his own. My English brother and his wife were killed recently in a flash flood in Texas when their car was swept off the road. Fortunately, Kyle, their son, wasn't with them at the time. I'm all the family he has now."

Sarah reached across the table and laid a hand over Faith's. "I'm sorry for your loss. I lost my sister not long ago, so I understand your grief."

"*Danki*. I had not seen my brother for many years. He fell in love with an English girl and left our faith. I've never met his son. I'm trying to adopt him, but the process is painfully slow."

Nettie finished dishing out the pie and handed the plate to Faith. "It will be a hard change for him coming from an *Englisch* life to live in an Amish home."

"I am worried about that. What if he says he doesn't want to live here?"

Sarah gave Faith an incredulous look. "What little boy wouldn't love to live on a farm?"

"One who is used to television and video games." Faith was giving voice to one of her biggest fears. That Kyle would hate living with her.

"To worry about such things is to borrow trouble," Nettie chided. "God is bringing this child into your life. He knows what is best for all of us."

"You're right. I will put my trust in Him." Faith took a bite of her pie and savored the sweet tart flavor and tender, flaky crust. Nettie Sutter really knew how to make good pie.

"Tell us about yourself," Katie prompted. "I hear you have some unusual animals."

"I have ten alpacas. I raise them for their fleece. I spin it into yarns. Once I get this house in order, I will start looking for a place to sell my work."

Sarah brightened. "I work at a fabric store and we sell many types of yarn. The store owner's name is Janet Mallory. You should speak to her."

"In Hope Springs?" Could it possibly be this easy to find a market for her work? Faith dared not get her hopes up.

"Yes, we are on Main Street, downtown. You can't miss it. It's called Needles and Pins. Janet is always looking for things made by the local Amish people to sell in her store. We get a fair amount of tourists in Hope Springs. Amish handmade items sell very well, although most of our yarn is bought by local Amish women for use at home."

Faith said, "I'm grateful for your suggestion. I will come in once I have my house in order."

Sarah leaned forward. "Is it true that your animal spit on Adrian? His brother, Ben, said he smelled as bad as a skunk."

Faith felt the heat rush to her cheeks. "Myrtle did spit on Adrian. I don't blame him for being upset."

Sarah laughed, a sweet light sound that made Faith smile, too. "I would have given anything to see Adrian lose his composure. What did he say?"

Faith crossed her arms over her chest and mimicked his deep stern voice. "Your creatures are eating my beans."

"*Ja,* that is just the way he talks." Sarah giggled again, then took another bite of her pie.

Faith couldn't let them think Adrian had been unkind. "He was upset, but he helped me catch them. Except for Myrtle, the others seem to like him. He's also been helping me build fences to keep them in."

Sarah sobered. "Adrian is coming over to help you build fences? That's interesting. He has stayed mainly to himself these past few years."

Faith's curiosity was piqued. Wanting to learn more about her stoic neighbor, she asked, "Why is that?"

Sarah glanced at the other women, then back to Faith. "Adrian's wife died shortly after their son was born. He raised the boy by himself. His son was his whole world. One afternoon, Adrian was walking home from his field that lies across the highway from his house. His son saw him coming and raced out to greet him. He ran right into the path of a car and was killed in front of Adrian."

Faith's heart twisted with pity knowing the pain he must have felt. "No parent should have to bury a child."

Nettie sighed heavily. "There is no greater sorrow. That is how we know God loves us. For He allowed His only son to die for our sins so that we may rejoice with Him in heaven for eternity."

From the tone of her voice and the sadness in her eyes, Faith knew that Nettie was speaking from firsthand experience. She said, "It is our solace to know they are waiting to greet us in heaven."

"Indeed it is," Nettie agreed.

Katie was the one to break the ensuing silence. "I have never seen an alpaca up close. May I take a look at yours?"

"Of course." Faith took pity on the expectant mother having to listen to such a somber conversation. Rising to her feet, she motioned for Katie to follow her. Nettie and Sarah deposited the dirty plates in the sink and quickly joined them.

Outside, they crossed the yard in a tight group. Nettie eyed the sad state of the barn. "You will need to find a strong husband to get this farm in shape. We have several bachelors in our church district who would make a good husband to you and a father to your nephew."

Quickly, Faith said, "I have no plans to marry again."

"Not even if the right fellow happens along?" Katie teased.

"I'm too old to remarry," Faith added firmly.

Nettie started laughing. "No, you aren't. I'm getting married in a few weeks. If I found someone at my age, you can, too. It is all up to God."

Katie asked Nettie a question about preparations for the upcoming nuptials, and the two women began an animated discussion.

Faith slowed her pace and hoped that would be the end of her part in the conversation, but Sarah shortened her stride and dropped back beside her. "Nettie is right. It's up to God."

"It is up to me, too. I see no need to marry again."

She felt Sarah's keen eyes studying her intently. Finally, Sarah said, "Your marriage wasn't a happy one? I understand. We won't speak of it again."

Faith could only wonder if Sarah's experience in marriage was the same.

As they rounded the barn, Faith saw her alpacas were all grazing except for Myrtle. She stood alone near the barn door. Faith called out to them. "Come here, babies. I have people who want to meet you."

They all raised their heads to look at her, but only Socks ventured close.

"Will they spit at us?" Katie asked.

"They only spit if they are startled. Sometimes they will spit at each other if they are annoyed, but for the most part they all get along."

"They are so cute," Katie gushed.

Faith had had the same reaction the first time she'd seen one. "They are wonderful animals. They are docile and they are quite smart."

"Which one spit on my cousin?" Sarah leaned her arms on the top of the gate.

Faith pointed. "That was Myrtle. She's the gray one standing by the barn door. She is expecting in a few weeks."

Katie started laughing. "I know just how she feels. Being pregnant makes me moody, too. Some days I feel like spitting at my husband. Poor Elam knows to stay out of my way when I get in a temper."

Nettie and Sarah joined in Katie's laughter. Myrtle moved as far away from the noise as she could get. She huddled by the corner of the barn and watched them all with a wary expression.

Faith felt a glimmer of hope begin to grow in her heart. She would enjoy having these women for friends. It seemed things were beginning to look up for her in this new place.

"Here you all are!"

Faith looked past Myrtle as a woman walked into view from around the corner of the barn. Myrtle took quick exception to the stranger coming so close. She spat and galloped to the far side of the pen, giving an alarm call that sent the entire herd milling in panic.

The middle-aged woman stood frozen with a shocked expression on her face as alpaca spit dripped from her chin.

Katie clasped her hands over her mouth. "Oh, no, not her."

"Who is it?" Faith asked, knowing full well she didn't want to hear the answer.

"The bishop's wife," Katie whispered.

"You should have seen the look on Esther Zook's face." Sarah started giggling again. "I'm sorry, I can't help it. It was the funniest thing. Poor Faith, I've never seen anyone so contrite."

Adrian, sitting in the corner of his living room, continued his pretense of reading the newspaper while he listened to his cousin regale his mother with her story. Sarah was a frequent visitor in his home. They had been close since they were children.

"What did you think of her?" his mother asked.

"Adrian's new neighbor or the bishop's wife?" Sarah began giggling again.

Glancing over top of the paper, Adrian saw his mother frown at Sarah's levity. "I meant Faith Martin."

Sarah shrugged. "She seems nice enough. She is certainly a hard worker."

His mother transferred her gaze to him. "It's a pity she is handicapped for there are several bachelors around who are on the lookout for a new wife."

Compelled to defend Faith, he said, "She walks with a barely noticeable limp. It isn't a handicap."

"I'm sure there is someone who is willing to overlook such a minor imperfection." She gave him a pointed stare.

He turned the page and ignored her broad hint. He wasn't on the lookout for a wife. His mother would eventually learn to accept that.

Sarah, a widow herself, rolled her eyes. "*Aenti* Linda, if you mean Toby Yoder and Ivan Stultz, I don't think they would mind a wife who walks with a limp. Not as long as she can cook and clean, mend clothes, run a farm and milk twenty cows twice a day while they spend their time gossiping at the feed store. Why, they would both be thrilled to have such a woman."

"You might be right," his mother admitted.

Adrian couldn't stay silent any longer. "Maybe she doesn't want to marry again. Did you think of that?"

"What woman doesn't want a husband and children of her own?" his mother countered.

"The love between a husband or wife doesn't die because one of them is with God. It lives on." He didn't care if she knew he was talking about himself.

Her gaze softened. "Of course not, but we can love more than one person."

I know. I loved a wife and a child and God took them both.

"Sarah hasn't remarried," he pointed out, keeping his painful thoughts to himself. His cousin ducked her head. Her smile vanished. He was sorry he'd brought the subject up. Sarah's husband had passed away from cancer over three years ago.

Glancing from Sarah back to Adrian, his mother gave him a fierce scowl. "Sarah has not closed her heart to love. It will find her again when God wills it. Hopefully, before she is too old to bear children."

He went back to his paper, knowing his mother would always have the last word.

Sarah said, "Faith doesn't have to worry about that. She already has a child on the way."

"What?" Adrian and his mother demanded together in shocked surprise.

Sarah couldn't keep a straight face. "She is adopting her brother's child."

"Well, that changes things a little," his mother mused. "Not all men want a wife and a child at the same time."

Sarah propped her elbows on the table. "Faith insists she won't marry again, and I believe she means it."

Linda waved aside her comment. "Nonsense. Once she has had the chance to meet a few of our fellows she'll change her mind. Let me think. Micah Beachy might be just the one. He's got a nice little farm over by Sugarcreek and he's never been married. I'll have to invite him over for a visit next month."

Intrigued by Sarah's comments, Adrian asked, "She specifically said she won't remarry? Does she intend to raise a child alone?"

Sarah turned in her seat to face Adrian. "*Ja*. What did you think of Faith when you met her?"

"I think she is going to have a hard time making a go of that farm. She doesn't have the money to hire help."

He understood Faith's reluctance to marry again. Suffering the pain of losing a spouse and child was more than anyone should have to bear. Loving someone meant risking that pain again. He wasn't willing to take that chance.

"The peaches in her orchard should be nearly ripe. If she sells her fruit, she'll be able to make some money, won't she?" Sarah asked.

Adrian shook his head. "The place is so overgrown, she'll have a hard time even getting to the fruit. Those trees haven't been pruned in twenty years. Most of them are so old they may not even bear fruit anymore. The peaches she does have will be small because no one thinned out the fruit when it was setting on."

"I told her to bring some of her yarns into Needles and Pins. I'm sure Janet will allow her to sell them there."

He turned the page of his paper. "It will take a lot of yarn to fix up that farm."

His mother left off cleaning the kitchen counter and began wiping down the table. "What kind of shape is the house in?"

Sarah brightened. "It's not too bad. I didn't see any water damage inside, so the roof must still be sound. But it was so grimy. It took us hours to get the walls and floors clean. Elam Sutter, Eli Imhoff and his two sons managed to get the outside of the house painted but not the barn. I'm afraid it's in need of a few repairs first."

"More than a few," Adrian added, unable to stay out of the conversation.

His mother folded her arms over her ample bosom. "Then everyone will have their work cut out for them. It is clear our sister is in need. We cannot turn our backs on her."

Folding his paper and laying it aside for good, Adrian said, "Do you really think everyone will feel the same way? She isn't even a member of our church. Clearly, she didn't make a good impression on the bishop's wife."

His mother waved aside his objection. "Esther Zook will get over being made a laughingstock. She won't hold our new neighbor to blame for the actions of her animals. Esther knows her Christian duty, and when she forgets it, her husband will remind her."

Adrian exchanged glances with Sarah. She obviously wasn't in total agreement with his mother. She knew Esther Zook's opinion could sway many of the women in the community if she chose to rebuff Faith.

He rose to his feet. Grabbing his straw hat from the peg beside the front door, he slapped it on his head.

"Where are you going?" His mother asked.

"To see a woman about some peaches."

He left the house and headed for the hay meadow that separated his property from Faith's farm as fast has his feet could carry him. With him out of the way, his mother could finish fussing in his kitchen and talk about him freely. Not that his presence ever stopped her.

She meant well, he knew that. He appreciated that she came by to cook and clean for him each week even though he didn't need her help. What he didn't like was her interference.

Twice he'd found Lovina and Gideon's clothes had been packed away in a trunk in the attic. He never said a word to his mother. He simply put the clothes back into the bureau beside his own. He wasn't ready to let go.

Adrian's rapid steps slowed as he approached Faith's house. He wasn't sure exactly what he wanted to say to her. He wasn't even sure why he'd come. As he neared the front of her house, he saw she had moved her spinning wheel onto the front porch, probably to take advantage of the cooler evening breezes.

Her head was bent over the wheel as she concentrated on her task. With deft fingers, she pulled fleece from a bundle into long slender strands. Her feet pumped the pedals and made the wheel fly, spinning the fleece rapidly into yarn that wound around a pair of spindles.

It wasn't so much the art of her work that caught his attention. It was the look on her face. The worry and pain he'd seen before were gone, replaced by an expression of serenity. A sweet, soft smile curved her lips. He caught snatches of a song she was humming. So this was how Faith Martin looked when she was happy.

He couldn't bring himself to interrupt. Instead, he leaned on her rickety gate and simply enjoyed watching her work.

He had once wished to see her smile. He had no idea the sight could steal his breath away.

As much as he wished to let her work in peace, he had come here for a reason.

Chapter Five

"You make that look easy."

Faith jerked upright, searching for the source of the voice that startled her. She relaxed when she caught sight of Adrian leaning against her front gate. What was he doing here this late in the day? Her fence was finished.

How long had he been watching her?

Did he disapprove of the song she'd been humming? Mose had always hated it when she'd sung or hummed.

Faith slowed her spinning wheel to a stop. It wasn't fair of her to compare Adrian to Mose. They were two very different men. Even from the small amount of time she'd spent with Adrian, she could see that. She had to learn to let go of the past.

She said, "It is easy when you find the right rhythm. What can I do for you this evening?"

"I have come with another proposition for you."

Disappointment stabbed her. He'd come to make another offer on her land. Was she foolhardy to hang on to her dream of a place of her own?

She gathered up her loose fleece and placed it back in a blue plastic laundry basket. "I am still not interested in selling my land."

"What about your peaches?" He opened the gate and walked to the foot of her steps.

She shifted her basket to her good hip. "You want to buy peaches from me?"

"Not exactly. I'm willing to harvest your fruit and sell it for shares."

Faith pondered his surprising offer. She already had more work to do than she could possibly get done before Kyle arrived. That was, if the adoption when through. Selling peaches hadn't entered her mind. She had thought only of canning some for herself.

The extra income would be most welcome if Adrian was willing to do the work. "What share would you be asking?"

"I was thinking of a seventy/thirty split."

That was generous. "Seventy for me, thirty for you?"

He cracked a smile as he shook his head. "*Nee*. I would be doing the majority of the work."

Maybe so, but she wasn't going to *give* her produce away. "The fruit is all mine. If you will do fifty/fifty, I'll consider it."

"The crop will go to waste if I don't pick it for you. In that case, you'll get nothing."

He spoke the truth and she knew it. "Very well, sixty/forty and we have a deal."

Nodding once, he said, "*Goot*. We have a deal."

She expected him to leave, but he didn't. The heat of the day had waned. A cool breeze slipped past her cheeks and rustled through the leaves of the trees beside the house. For her, evenings were the best time of the day. She said, "I have some sweet tea made. Would you care for a glass?"

He hesitated. She thought he would refuse, but to her surprise, he said, "*Ja*. That would be nice."

"Let me put my fleece away and I'll be right back with some."

She hurried inside the house, feeling strangely lighthearted. When she came out again, he was sitting on the bottom step. After handing him the glass of tea, she awkwardly sank down on the step beside him. His hand shot toward her. She flinched away before she could stop herself.

He withdrew his hand slowly. The frown she was beginning to know so well settled on his face. He regarded her with a quizzical look in his eyes.

Faith stretched her bad leg out in front of her and tried to pretend nothing had happened. "I hope the tea is sweet enough."

"Does it hurt much?" he asked softly.

She rubbed her thigh and swallowed hard, uncomfortable with his sympathy. "Not as much as it used to."

"How did it happen? If you don't mind my asking?"

She didn't mind talking about the accident. It was talking about her marriage that she shied away from. "A pickup struck our buggy when we were on our way home from church."

Adrian took a sip of his tea, then stared out across the yard. "Is that how your husband died?"

"Mose was killed instantly." Faith stared into her glass as she relived those painful days.

"My son was struck and killed by a car. The English, they go so fast in their big machines. What in their lives makes them rush so?"

"It seems to me they are afraid they will miss something important."

"What was more important than my son's life?"

"Nothing." She wanted so much to reach out and comfort him. What would he think if she did? She tightened her grip on her glass.

After a moment of silence, Adrian shook off his somber mood. "I understand Myrtle met the bishop's wife today."

Faith pressed a hand to her cheek. "Please don't remind me. It was horrible."

"Sarah thought it was quite funny."

Faith cast him a sideways glance. "That was the worst part. Everyone was trying so hard not to laugh while I was stuttering my apologies."

"I'm sure you told her alpaca spit will brush off when it dries."

"Of course I did."

"Did you also mention how long the smell lingers?"

"I suggested she wash her clothes with baking soda to cut the odor as soon as she got home."

"I don't recall you giving me that information."

She tried to look innocent. "Didn't I?"

"*Nee.* I will assume you were too worried about your animals to pass along that important piece of advice."

"*Ja*, don't think for a minute it was because you were scowling so fiercely that the words flew out of my head."

"Did I frighten you that day?"

She shrugged. "A little."

"Are you frightened of me now?"

She knew he was referring to the way she had flinched from him a few moments ago. She stared down at the glass in her hand, avoiding his gaze. "You have been most helpful to me. I could not ask for a better neighbor."

It wasn't an answer to his question, but it was the best she could do. He said nothing more. The sounds of cicadas rose and fell as they started their noisy evening songs. As abruptly as it started, their song stopped, and the silence stretched on for another awkward minute.

Faith racked her mind for something to say, but Adrian beat her to it. "I will go through your orchard on Wednesday and see if the fruit is ripe enough for picking."

"It's a mess. There are downed branches and dead trees all through it."

"We had a bad ice storm a few years back. I imagine most of the damage is from that. However, many of the trees are getting old. Peach trees only live about twenty years and these were planted at least that long ago."

"Do you know if they are freestone or clingstone peaches?"

A hint of a grin tugged at the corner of his lips. "The ones I snitched as a *kinder* were all freestone and extra sweet."

She smiled at his confession. It was easy to imagine him as a mischievous child. "*Goot.* Those are the best kind for selling at market."

Faith smoothed her skirt with one hand. It should have felt strange to be sitting beside Adrian and discussing the work that needed to be done on the farm, but it didn't. It felt comfortable. It was only when the conversation turned personal that she grew uncomfortable.

The shadows had grown long, and the cicadas resumed their evening serenade. Adrian finished his drink and rose to his feet. "It's getting late. I should go home."

Faith tried to stand but didn't quite make it. Embarrassed, she gathered herself to try again. Adrian stepped close and held out his hand to aid her.

Faith's heart began hammering so hard she was sure he could hear it. Fear made her mouth dry. Adrian wasn't Mose. She didn't have to be afraid anymore. They were brave words but hard to live by. She ignored his hand and pulled herself upright using the railing.

Adrian saw the change that came over Faith when he offered his hand. Was it pride that made her struggle to her feet alone? He didn't think so.

He saw the flash of fear in her eyes, although she hid it quickly. What reason would Faith Martin have to fear him?

He let his hand fall back against his side. If his presence was unwelcome, he would not force it upon her. "I will see you Wednesday, then."

She twisted her hands together as she avoided looking at him. "I may not be here. I'm taking my yarns into town. Your cousin Sarah was kind enough to invite me to bring my work into her shop. After that, I will be here, but I'm expecting the social worker from the adoption agency. I'm trying to adopt my brother's child."

Was that why she seemed so worried? Was she afraid her adoption wouldn't go through? He tried to picture her with a babe in her arms. She would make a good mother.

He said, "You don't need to be here while I survey your orchard. We can discuss what I find another time. I promise I won't eat up your profits."

She smiled halfheartedly at his humor. He wanted more. He wanted a real smile from her. "How are your beasts adjusting to their new home?"

"They seem quite happy in the pen you built for them. Thank you for your help with that. They are growing fat on the thick grass in the orchard."

"Will I disturb them working in there?"

"I do not think so. They may disturb you for they are quite curious. You're likely to find them underfoot and investigating everything you do."

He nodded toward the barn. "Has your expectant mother had her calf?"

"A baby alpaca is called a cria, not a calf." She relaxed as she talked about her animals. The haunted look faded from her eyes.

"Cria." He rolled the unfamiliar word on his tongue. "Has Myrtle had her cria?"

"Not yet. I think it will be few more weeks before she becomes a mother again."

"This is not her first babe?"

"Bandit and Baby Face are both her offspring."

"You have chosen unusual names for your unusual creatures."

"My husband and I rented a farm from an English family when we lived in Missouri. I let their daughter name all the new babies."

"You will be able to name this one yourself."

She glanced shyly in his direction. "Perhaps I will give you the honor."

He stroked his beard as he considered her offer. "I could name it for its mother. *Shmakkich.*"

"Smelly? I will not call my new baby Smelly."

"Then you must find a better name yourself for that is my only suggestion." He handed her his empty glass.

She took it without hesitation. Her eyes crinkled with humor. "I did not think you would shirk from a difficult task."

"A challenge, is it? Very well, I shall name it Stinky."

"Nee." She shook her head.

"Foul Breath."

Faith giggled. *"Nee.* I will not call any creature Foul Breath. If that's the best you can do, it will remain nameless."

Her smile was back and Adrian was content. "I shall give it some more consideration. Good night, Faith Martin."

"Guten nacht, Adrian."

He started toward home but stopped a few yards away. Turning around, he called out, "What about Skunk?"

"Nee! That's the worst name ever."

"But what if it's black with a white stripe down its back?"

"Not even then. Be off with you, foolish fellow." She shooed him away with one hand, but she was smiling.

It wasn't until he was nearly home that he realized he was still smiling, too.

Faith guided Copper onto the highway and headed toward Hope Springs. The horse kept to a brisk trot, but it wasn't long before several cars were backed up behind Faith's buggy waiting to pass her on the next open stretch of road. The driver of the first car that went around her gave her a friendly wave. The second car drew alongside but didn't pass. When Faith glanced their way, she saw the passenger had the window rolled down and was aiming the camera in her direction.

Faith quickly turned her face away. No matter which Amish community she lived in, it was always the same. There were always a few tourists who just had to snap a photograph of an Amish person. They never seemed to realize it was rude.

The second car sped away, and Faith was free to enjoy the green rolling countryside. It was easy to see how fertile the land was as she passed farm after farm with tall cornfields and fat cattle grazing near the roadside.

The outskirts of Hope Springs came into view after several miles. Faith had no trouble finding her way to the fabric store. She pulled Copper to a stop in the parking lot beside three other buggies.

As soon as she pushed open the front door of Needles and Pins, she was greeted with the scent of a floral and vanilla potpourri and the sound of chimes. The store was small, but it was crammed from floor to ceiling with bolts of fabric in every color. At the rear of the store a white-haired woman stood behind the counter. She looked up from her work and smiled in greeting.

"Welcome to Needles and Pins. Is there something I can help you with?"

Faith worked to quell the nervousness making her stomach queasy. She needed to find a market for her work as soon as possible. One of the things Kyle's social worker would be looking at was her financial situation. Faith needed proof that she earned enough to care for a child. Sending up a quick prayer, she said, "I'm looking for Janet."

"Then look no further. I'm she."

Faith approached the counter. After introducing herself, she opened her bag and pulled out a sample of her yarn. "Would you be interested in purchasing some hand-spun baby alpaca yarn?"

"I might be." Janet took the skein to examine closely.

"The black color is natural. It's from one of my crias."

Janet looked up in surprise. "You raise your own alpacas?"

"*Ja,* I have ten animals. Some are white, I have one black, several grays and two that are butternut-brown. I can die the wool for you if you have customers that want a particular color. It's very soft yarn and very strong." Faith forced herself to stop babbling.

Running her hand over the skein, Janet said, "I can see this is quality work, Mrs. Martin. I would be interested in buying all you have in black and dark gray. I'm not sure about the other colors. Perhaps I will take a few of them and see how they sell."

Faith struggled to hide her excitement. She had prayed to make a big sale today, and her prayers were being answered.

Janet continued, "If you are interested, I could post your yarn for sale on my website. I get a fair number of internet orders."

"That would be *goot, danki*." This was better yet.

Faith sorted her yarns for Janet and pocketed the money

with a happy heart. She was preparing to leave when Sarah came out from the back room. Smiling, Sarah came forward carrying several large bolts of powder-blue material. "Faith, how are you? Have you brought in your yarn?"

"*Ja*. Janet was kind enough to purchase several dozen skeins. If they sell well, she will buy more."

Sarah leaned close. "I will do my best to steer our customers toward them."

"I appreciate that."

"I have been instructed by Nettie Sutter to invite you to our widow's meeting on Friday night."

Such meetings were common in Amish communities where widows sought to remain active and productive members of the community even into old age. Faith had been a member of such a group in her last church district.

As much as she wanted to say yes, Faith didn't have time to devote to social visits. "Perhaps I can join you when I've settled in."

"Fair enough. We are finishing two quilts that will be auctioned off next month. We help support an orphanage in Haiti with the money we raise and we give to the church to help our members who have medical bills and such. Several times a year we hold a large auction. Some of the women in our church have started a co-op to help members market and sell their work."

"I'm not much of a hand at quilting," Faith admitted.

"Don't worry, we will find something for you to do. We meet at the home of Naomi Wadler. Her daughter and son-in-law run the Wadler Inn and Shoofly Pie Café. You passed by it on your way in town. Naomi's home is behind the inn."

Faith remembered the Swiss-chalet-style inn at the edge of town. "What time are the meetings held?"

"Five o'clock."

"I look forward to the day I can meet with you."

"Wonderful. Have you decided to join our church?"

"I plan to ask the bishop about it soon."

"I must warn you that once you are accepted, you will be fair game as far as Adrian's mother is concerned."

Perplexed, Faith asked, "Why do I need a warning about his mother?"

"*Aenti* Linda fancies herself a matchmaker. Adrian and I are her only current failures. I admit she does have a knack for putting the right people together. You will provide her a new challenge. Hopefully, I can get a break from chance meetings and uncomfortable suppers at her house where I feel like a prize hen on display."

Faith shook her head. "She may match-make all she wants. I have no intention of marrying again."

"That is exactly what Adrian says."

Faith began to rearrange the yarns left in her basket. "It is a shame he feels that way. He would make a good husband."

"He's a handsome fellow, I'll give him that."

"He's much more than that. He's kind and generous, strong and hardworking. He's everything a woman could desire in a mate."

As soon as she realized she was rambling, Faith looked up in embarrassment. Sarah stared back with a look of compassion on her face.

Faith wanted to sink through the floor. She hadn't realized how much she had come to admire Adrian or how much she wanted to be admired by him.

Sarah reached out and laid a hand on Faith's arm. "Adrian still grieves deeply for his wife and son. He says the love he holds in his heart for his first wife doesn't leave room for another. He speaks with conviction when he says he will never love again. A woman who sets her heart on my cousin is likely to find heartache instead."

* * *

Adrian started his assessment of Faith's orchard under the close supervision of her alpacas. The herd followed him everywhere, observing his activity with wide curious eyes. Their heads bobbed back and forth on their long necks as they tried to figure out what he was up to.

Before long, the group grew tired of simply watching him. They began a new game, bounding away, then racing back at him, dodging aside at the last second to avoid a collision. Soon, several mock battles broke out between the youngsters. They chased each other around the trees, kicking and knocking their long necks into one another. Socks and Baby Face reared up and began a boxing match as they hopped about on their rear legs.

Adrian chuckled at their antics. It was like being surrounded by five-foot-tall puppies. He began to understand Faith's attraction to them. They were adorable. Like their owner.

Only Myrtle refused to join the fun. She spit at those brave or foolish enough to encroach on her space. Adrian had no trouble staying away from her.

He finished his task and was letting himself out the gate to the orchard when he saw Faith returning. His spirits lifted instantly. She was sure to smile when he recounted her animals' antics.

She drew her horse to a stop beside the barn door. He held the mare's headstall as Faith descended from the buggy. "Did you sell all your yarn?" he asked.

She pulled a large hamper from the backseat. "Not all of it but a large portion. I hope you have some good news about my orchard."

"You have very curious animals prowling out there."

Her face filled with concern. "Did they give you trouble?"

"I was able to dodge their charges and most of the spit."

"I will wash your shirt if need be."

"*Nee,* I'm only teasing. You have about ten trees that should be cut down. They are too old and diseased to bear fruit. They can be cut up and stacked for firewood. They should dry out enough through the fall to burn well this winter."

Faith set her basket on the ground. "Should I replant more peach trees in their place?"

"If I were you, I'd diversify with some plum and apple trees. Since they flower at different times, you will be less likely to lose the entire crop if we get a late freeze in the spring.

Her eyebrows shot up. "So you think I will be here in the spring? Have you decided I can make a go of this place?"

"You have made a good start," he admitted.

"Only because you've done the majority of the outside work. Your help has been a godsend."

Adrian grew uncomfortable with her gratitude. He hadn't started out to help her earn a living. He'd had his own selfish reasons for doing the work needed. He had hoped she would sell her farm to him.

Did he still want her to leave?

No…and yes.

He hadn't once thought of Lovina all through this day. He'd thought only of what Faith would say, what would make her smile. Faith made him forget his pain.

He didn't want to feel this sense of wonder when she was near, but he did. Seeing her smile shouldn't make him happy, but it did.

Adrian turned away and started to unhitch the horse. Faith made him feel things he didn't want to feel. Things that had died in him when Lovina died.

Faith said, "I can manage. I'm sure you have your own work to see to."

"I've wasted the best part of the day here. I might as well stable your horse. It won't take that much longer." His voice sounded unnaturally harsh even to his own ears.

Faith took a step back and ducked her head. "I should get these things up to the house. The social worker will be here soon."

As she hurried away, Adrian could've kicked himself for stripping the happiness from her eyes. Had he been wrapped up in his own grief so long that he'd forgotten how to be kind?

Chapter Six

Faith put her yarns and baskets away and worked up the courage to return to the barn. She had upset Adrian, but she didn't know how. Was it something she said? He'd done too much for her to let him go away angry.

She paused at the kitchen door, remembering Adrian as he had first appeared to her, dark and scowling. In spite of his fierce appearance, he'd been nothing but kind to her. She had come to care for him, to see him as a friend, yet she had scurried away from his displeasure like a sheep running from the wolf. Why was it still so hard to stand up for herself?

Because I'm afraid.

Was Adrian's kindness only an act or did her old fear make her suspect evil where it didn't exist? If she couldn't be sure, how could she do business with him, accept his help, allow him into her life?

Learning to trust again was harder than relearning to walk had been. Perhaps that was the reason God had brought her to this place. Because she had to begin somewhere. If this was her first test, she had failed miserably.

No, that wasn't true because she wanted to trust Adrian. The real problem was that she no longer trusted her own judgment.

Dear Father in heaven, give me strength and wisdom. Let me not judge others lest I be judged in return. Help me to see the good in men and not suspect evil.

Bolstered by her prayer, Faith left the house, crossed the yard and pulled open the barn door. Adrian was busy forking hay into Copper's stall. He hadn't seen her return.

Unobserved, Faith took a moment to admire the way he made the work look easy. His strong arms and shoulders drove the fork deep into the hay and lifted a bundle with ease. Beneath the sweat-dampened shirt he wore, she could see the muscles tightening and rippling across his back. Her breath quickened as she realized she wasn't seeing him as a friend should. Embarrassed, she looked away.

He was a strong, handsome man, and he was proving himself to be a good friend and neighbor. That was all. She wouldn't let it be anything else.

He caught sight of her. "I'll be done in a minute."

He didn't seem angry now. She took a step closer. "I'm sorry I upset you earlier."

His eyes widened in surprise. "You did nothing to upset me. I'm the one who should be sorry. I let my ill humor ruin your day. That was wrong. The help I gave you was for selfish reasons. Please forgive me."

"You are forgiven. For what selfish reason have you worked here day in and day out?"

He hesitated, then sighed. "I thought if you couldn't make a go of this farm, I could buy it from you. The work that I've done here would have had to be done anyway when I took over."

"I see. Thank you for telling me this."

"I no longer think you will fail, Faith Martin. You have the will to succeed, and as you once told me, you aren't afraid of hard work.

A sound outside drew her attention. Faith's heart leaped

into her throat when she saw the automobile pulling to a stop in front of her house. In the front seat she could see a woman surveying the property. "That must be Mrs. Taylor, Kyle's social worker. What do I do?"

Adrian came to stand beside her. Gently, he said, "Go and welcome her."

His simple reply made her realize how silly she was being. "Kyle was raised in an *Englisch* home. I'm worried that this *Englisch* woman won't think he belongs in an Amish home."

"You cannot discover the answers you seek by hiding here in the barn."

"Are you sure?"

"*Ja,* I'm pretty sure." He smiled and motioned her toward the door. "Go."

Gathering her courage, Faith walked out of the barn and toward the car, knowing this was the moment she had been dreading and praying for. She had had several letters from Mrs. Taylor, but she had no idea what to expect from the *Englisch* social worker.

The car door opened, and a tall, slender young woman got out. She wore a plum-colored suit and matching high-heeled shoes. Her hair was short and dark. It curled tightly against her skull. She held a briefcase in one hand.

Faith managed a smile. "*Velkumm.* Are you a Mrs. Taylor?"

"I'm afraid Mrs. Taylor no longer works for our agency. I'm Miss Watkins. Caroline Watkins. Are you Faith Miller?"

"Martin," Faith corrected her.

"My apologies." Caroline's gaze was fastened on Adrian standing by the barn. "Is that Mr. Martin?"

"No. That is my neighbor, Adrian Lapp. I am a widow. I thought you knew that."

"I'm sure it was in the file. I apologize if I sound unprepared.

I've been swamped with work. Yours is my third home visit this week. Mrs. Taylor left on very short notice and I'm playing catch-up."

"Do come in the house." Faith gestured toward the front door.

Would her home pass inspection? Was it clean enough? Was it big enough? Would Faith pass as a prospective parent, or would this woman decide she didn't deserve her nephew? Worry gnawed at her insides. Exactly what would this home study entail?

Inside the house, Faith led the way to the living room. It was sparely furnished with a small sofa placed in front of a pair of tall windows. Two reading chairs flanked the couch. A small bookcase sat against the wall opposite the windows. Miss Watkins settled herself on the sofa while Faith perched on the edge of a chair facing her.

Miss Watkins must have seen the concern Faith was trying to conceal. "Please don't be nervous, Mrs. Martin. I'm here to make sure your home is a suitable, safe place for your nephew, not to pass judgment on your housekeeping or personal tastes."

"I am Kyle's only family. What could be more suitable than that?"

"I agree it is almost always best to place a child with a relative, but placing a child in a safe and loving home is our top priority, even if that means placing them with someone other than a blood relative."

The social worker searched through her papers. "First, I need to see two forms of identification. I have to make sure I'm talking to the right person. Confidentiality laws and all that, you know. Your driver's license and a Social Security card will be fine."

"I do not have such documents."

Miss Watkins frowned. "You don't have a Social Security card?"

"I do not. The Amish do not believe in Social Security. It is the responsibility of everyone to care for the sick and elderly. We do not depend upon the government to do that for us. I do have my birth certificate and my marriage license, if that will do?"

Faith rose from the chair and crossed to the small bookcase in the corner. She opened her Bible and took out several pieces of paper and handed them to the social worker.

"Under the circumstances, I think these will be fine. Today, I'd like to gather some information about your background, family life, child care expectations and about your parenting philosophy. I know you must be frustrated at having to repeat some of this process since you began your adoption in Missouri, but now that you are in Ohio, you will have to abide by Ohio law."

"I understand my move came at a bad time, but it couldn't be helped."

"I will do what I can to expedite your home study. A few things won't have to be repeated. Your background check and criminal search records have been forwarded to us by the Missouri authorities."

"I only wish to have Kyle with me as soon as possible. He has been with strangers for two months."

Miss Watkins opened a folder. "Kyle King is in foster care in Texas, is that right?"

Faith nodded.

"And you've not been to visit him, is that correct?"

"I've spoken to him on the phone several times and written letters to him twice a week, every week, but I've been unable to travel to Texas." It wasn't much, but it was all she could do for now.

"I will admit I know very little about the Amish, so please

forgive my ignorance. You are the first Amish client I've worked with. I understand you do not use electricity."

"We do not."

"And you have no phone and no car."

"There is a phone shack at the end of the lane that I and my Amish neighbors may use. It is permitted for work and for emergencies. I have a horse and buggy for ordinary travel, but I may hire a driver if I must travel a long distance."

"I'll make a note of that. After our interview, I'll make a brief safety inspection of your home. Typically, this first visit lasts from three to four hours.

"Four hours?" Faith thought of all the work that she had waiting for her.

"Yes. Is that a problem?"

"*Nee,* of course not."

"If I can't gather all I need today I will schedule a follow-up visit. I don't see a statement from your doctor. Did you receive the paperwork we sent you?"

"I haven't had a chance to schedule an appointment."

Miss Watkins frowned. "Ohio law is very clear on this. In order to adopt a child, you must be in good health."

"I am. My limp is the result of an accident, not an illness. I'll take care of it this week." A doctor's visit was another expense Faith didn't need. The money from her yarn sales wouldn't go far.

"All right. Let's get started. Are there any other adults or children living in this home?"

"*Nee.*"

"Do you have adequate room to house a child?"

"*Ja,* this house has four bedrooms upstairs, although I don't yet have a bed for Kyle."

Miss Watkins jotted down some notes. "I will have to see all the accommodations prior to his arrival. Do you suffer from any physical or mental illnesses?"

"Only the limp you see."

"What is the reason for your disability?"

"I was injured when a pickup struck our buggy. My husband was killed."

"I'm sorry for your loss."

"It was God's will." Faith couldn't pretend there was sorrow in her heart, for there was none. Only relief and guilt for not loving Mose as a wife should.

"Do you have a history of alcohol, drug or substance abuse, even if it did not result in an arrest?"

"*Nee.*"

"Do you have a history of child abuse, even if it was not reported?"

"*Nee.*"

"Do you have a history of domestic violence, even if it did not result in an arrest or conviction?"

Faith's heart jumped to her throat. Would Mose reach out from the grave and snatch away her only chance to raise a child? She couldn't let that happen.

Never again would she place herself, or Kyle, in such a situation. She answered carefully for she didn't want to lie. "I have never abused anyone nor have I been accused of such behavior."

"Have you ever been rejected for adoption or foster care?"

Faith relaxed. "I have not."

For the next several hours, Faith answered all the questions put to her. Finally, Miss Watkins said, "Why don't we take a break and you can show me the house."

"Of course. I have only recently moved in. There is still much work to be done."

"I understand. Let's start with the kitchen."

Faith led the way. Miss Watkins made notes as she walked. To Faith, it seemed that she took note of every flaw, every uneven floorboard and even the stains on the wall behind the stove. The house might not be perfect, but it was a roof over her head.

In the kitchen, Miss Watkins went straight to the refrigerator and opened the door. The shelves were bare except for a few staples—butter, eggs and some bacon. She turned to Faith. "You don't have much in the way of food here."

"I have only myself to cook for. I don't need much."

"Will feeding a growing boy be difficult for you?"

"Not at all. Come. I will show you the cellar." Faith took a lamp from inside the cupboard and lit the wick. Opening a door at the back of kitchen, Faith descended the steps, cautioning Miss Watkins to use the handrail.

Down in the cool, damp cellar, Faith raised her lamp to show shelves full of canned fruits, vegetables and meats. It had taken her two solid days to clean out the cellar, repair the shelves and stock them. "I brought most of this with me from my previous home in Missouri. Some of my new neighbors have brought more as gifts."

"Impressive. Can we go back upstairs now?"

Clearly, Miss Watkins didn't care to remain in a small dark space. She frowned as she eyed the lamp Faith held. "I have some concern about the use of kerosene lamps around a small child."

"Amish children are all taught how to use lamps safely."

"Open flames are very dangerous. You will have to provide an alternate source of light."

"Would battery-powered lights be acceptable?"

"Absolutely."

"Then I shall purchase some." Faith smiled. More expenses.

After leaving the cellar, Faith gave the social worker a tour of the yard and outbuildings. Once again, Miss Watkins was scribbling furiously in her notebook. The alpaca herd came to the fence to observe the newcomer. Faith assured the social worker that they were not dangerous animals, but she gave Myrtle a wide berth. The rest of the herd remained well behaved, much to her relief.

Back in the house, Miss Watkins gathered together her papers. She closed her briefcase and handed Faith two additional pieces of paper. "I think that will do it for today. As far as paperwork goes, you will need to complete the health summary and you will need to have a fire safety inspection."

Was that a free service or was it something else she would have to pay for?

Miss Watkins held out her hand. "I will be back the same time next week. Hopefully, you will have everything completed by then."

Twisting her hands together, Faith asked, "What if I don't?"

"If there are deficiencies, it does not automatically mean you can't adopt your nephew. It simply means that these are things we will have to work on."

As Faith watched the social worker drive away, she had no idea if she had passed inspection or not.

Why should they feel she deserved a child if God had not seen fit to answer her prayers for one? Simply because she was Kyle's aunt didn't mean she was the best person to raise him.

Glancing toward the orchard, she wondered if Adrian was still working out there or if he had gone home. An intense need to see him took hold of her.

Faith let herself through the gate behind the barn. Only Socks was grazing near the building. The rest of the herd had disappeared. Lifting her head, Socks ambled slowly in Faith's direction. When she reached Faith, she stopped and rubbed her head against Faith's side.

"What are you doing here all by yourself? Where is the

rest of the herd?" Faith peered into the trees but couldn't see the animals. Giving Socks a quick pat, Faith headed deeper into the orchard.

She hadn't gone far when she spotted the rest of the group. They were clustered around a single tree and all gazing upward. A ladder stood propped against the trunk. She could just make out Adrian's legs halfway up the rungs.

She was startled when he called out, "How did it go?"

"I wish I knew."

A large, dead branch came crashing to the ground, sending the alpacas dashing in circles before they clustered again beside the ladder. Adrian descended from the tree. "How soon will you know if your nephew can live with you?"

"For all the hurry, hurry, hurry in *Englisch* lives, their child placement process moves slowly. If all goes well, it may be two or three weeks."

"Where is he until then?"

"In a foster home."

"I'm sure they are taking good care of him."

"I pray so."

If the *Englisch* woman didn't find Faith acceptable, what would happen to Kyle? Was there someone else waiting and longing to adopt a child the way she was? Perhaps they deserved him more than she did.

She looked at Adrian. "Am I doing the right thing trying to bring an *Englisch* child here?"

"Why would you ask that?"

She crossed her arms and hugged herself as if she were cold. "Because in all the years I was married, God never saw fit to give me a child of my own."

Adrian heard the pain in Faith's voice. He saw the disappointment and loss in her eyes. He wanted to take her pain away, but he didn't know how. "Will you love this child?"

"I will."

"Then you are doing the right thing."

"If only I could be so sure. I must put my trust in God."

He said, *"And they that know thy name will put their trust in thee: for thou, LORD, hast not forsaken them that seek thee.* Psalm 9:10."

"You are so very right. He has not forsaken me."

Adrian wasn't sure why that particular Bible verse popped into his head. God had turned away from him. He had been forsaken. Faith, too, had suffered a great loss, and yet she still drew comfort and hope from God's word.

Why was her faith so strong when his was so weak?

Chapter Seven

On Sunday morning, Faith turned Copper off the highway and onto a farm lane two miles north of her home. At the edge of the road a homemade white sign with a black anvil painted on it said, "Horse Shoeing. Closed Wednesdays."

The church service was being held at the farm of Eli Imhoff, the local blacksmith, and the generous neighbor who, along with his sons, had painted the outside of her house.

Overhead, low gray clouds scuttled northward. The overcast sky was a welcome relief from the oppressive heat of the past few days, but the clouds were hanging on to any rain they held. Hopefully, any showers would remain at bay until after she was back home again.

At the other end of the long lane, Faith saw a two-story white house with a smaller *dawdy haus* built at a right angle from the main home. Both the grandfather house and the main house had pretty porches with white railings and wide steps. Three large birdhouses sat atop poles around the yard ringed with flower beds. Someday, her home would look like this.

Across an expanse of grass now crowded with buggies and groups of churchgoers stood a big red barn. In the corral, a pair of caramel-colored draft horses shared round hay bales with several dozen smaller horses. Copper whinnied a greeting. Several horses in the corral replied in kind.

A man came forward to take the reins from Faith. He tipped his black hat. "Good morning, *Frau*. I am Jonathan Dressler. I will take care of your horse." Although he looked Amish, he spoke in flawless English without a hint of the Pennsylvania Dutch accent she was accustomed to hearing.

"*Danki,* Jonathan." Faith stepped down from her vehicle and smoothed her skirt. Her stomach churned with nervous butterflies. More anxious than she cared to admit, she pulled a picnic hamper from beneath the front seat and stood rooted to the spot.

He pointed toward the farmhouse. "You may take your basket to the house. Karen Imhoff is in charge of the food today. It's nice to meet another newcomer to the community. Thanks to you, I'm no longer the new kid on the block."

"You are new here, too?"

"Yes. I guess I should say, *ja.*"

"You are *Englisch,* yet you dress plain."

"God has called me to live this simple life. Every day I give thanks that He led me to this place."

The smile on his handsome face was contagious. She asked, "Have you any advice to share with this newcomer?"

"The people of Hope Springs are wonderful, welcoming souls."

As they were speaking, another horse and buggy came trotting into the yard. She recognized Adrian at the reins. With him were an older man and woman, two younger women in their early twenties, and a teenage boy.

Jonathan said, "I best get back to work, but I have to ask you one question. Did your alpaca really spit on the bishop's wife?"

Her shoulders slumped. "Has everyone heard of this?"

Jonathan chuckled. "It is not kind of me to say, but your alpaca sounds like a wonderful judge of character."

He laughed again as he unhitched Copper and led her to the corral.

Faith's heart sank to a new low. She would have to attend services several times in this church district before the congregation would be asked to accept her. Neither the bishop nor his wife was likely to want a new member who'd made Mrs. Zook a laughingstock.

Faith looked toward the house and saw the women from Adrian's buggy join a large group of women gathered on the porch. She recognized the bishop's wife standing among them. All eyes were turned in her direction.

She wanted to run home and hide.

"If I were you, I'd go in with my head up and smile as if nothing were wrong."

Faith glanced over her shoulder and saw Adrian unhooking his horse from the buggy. He wasn't looking at her, but she knew he was talking to her. There was no one else around.

He patted his horse's flank and spoke again, just as softly. "She will appear mean and petty if she snubs you when you are offering friendship, but if she senses fear, she won't have any trouble ignoring you. The other women will follow her lead."

"I should walk up to her and pretend my animal didn't spit in her face, is that what you suggest?"

"You have already apologized for that, haven't you?"

"More than once."

"Then it's over. Go, before they start to think you're *naerfich.*"

She was nervous. But he was right, bless the man. His encouragement was exactly what she needed. Raising her chin, Faith limped forward and pasted a smile on her face.

As she approached the house, she nodded to Mrs. Zook.

"Good morning. The Lord has blessed us with a fine morning, has He not? I look forward to hearing your husband's preaching for I hear God has graced him with a wonderful understanding of the Bible."

Mrs. Zook's smile wasn't overly warm, but at least she didn't cut Faith dead. She inclined her head slightly. "My husband speaks as God moves him. Joseph takes no credit for himself."

"That is as it should be. Where shall I put this?" Faith patted her basket, glad her voice wasn't shaking for her fingers were ice cold.

A second woman spoke up. "Inside. Karen Imhoff will show you where she wants things."

Faith nodded her thanks, pulled open the front door and went inside with a huge sigh of relief. Behind her she heard the women's lowered voices begin to buzz. She knew they were discussing her. Unfortunately, she couldn't make out what they were saying.

Inside the kitchen, Faith was thrilled to see Nettie, Sarah and Katie at work arranging the food on the counters and long tables set up against the walls. Everything appeared ready for the meal the congregation would share after the service was finished.

A tall, slender woman came in from a back room with a box of glasses. She added them to the table where the plates were stacked. Her eyes lit with mischief when she spied Faith. She said, "Hello. I'm Karen Imhoff. You must be Faith Martin. I have been hearing so much about you."

Faith gave a quick glance around the room and saw Sarah and Katie trying to hide their grins. She looked back at Karen. "*Ja,* I am the one with the spitting alpaca."

Sarah and Katie dissolved into giggles. Nettie gave them both a stern look. The young women quickly pulled themselves together.

Karen said, "I hope you enjoy the service today. We are always glad to see new faces."

The front door opened and Jonathan stuck his head in. He said, "Everyone is here now."

Faith noticed the way his gaze rested on Karen. There was a softness in his eyes that bespoke great affection.

"*Danki,* Jonathan," Karen replied. "We will be there shortly." There was no mistaking the love that flowed between them.

What would it be like, Faith wondered, to love wholeheartedly and be loved in return?

Jonathan started to close the door but stopped as a little girl of about nine slipped beneath his arm and into the kitchen.

After he closed the door, Faith said, "Jonathan is a most unusual young man. I have never known an *Englisch* person to join our faith."

Smiling fondly, Katie folded her hands atop her bulging tummy. "You should have Karen tell you the whole story of how Jonathan came to be with us. It is the most romantic tale."

"I should tell it. I saw him first," the little girl declared. She was the spitting image of Karen and clearly not shy.

Karen laid a hand on the child's head. "You are forgetting your manners, Anna. This is Faith Martin. She is new to Hope Springs, and we must make her welcome. Faith, this is my sister, Anna."

Faith smiled at her. "I'm pleased to meet you, and I'm dying to hear the story."

Anna eagerly launched into her tale. "Just before Christmas, Karen was taking us to school. I looked out the buggy window and I saw a dead man in the ditch. Only, he wasn't dead. He was only hurt, but bad. God made him forget who he was, so we called him John. He stayed with us until God let him remember his name. And now he knows who he is and he wants to marry my sister."

Anna grinned broadly, Karen blushed rosy red and the rest of the women grinned.

Karen cleared her throat. "That about sums it up."

Nettie said, "It's almost time for the service to start. Girls, take Faith down to the barn. I'll be there shortly."

"I'll show you the way," Anna said as she bounced toward the door.

Outside, the solidly overcast sky gave way to intermittent sunshine. The women followed Anna to the far side of the barn where a sloping earthen ramp led to the barn's loft. The huge doors had been propped open to catch the cool morning breeze.

Inside, rows of wooden benches in the large hayloft were filled with worshipers, men on one side of a center aisle, women on the other, all waiting for the church service to begin. Faith took a place beside Sarah, Karen and Katie. Anna wiggled her way in between Faith and Karen.

Glancing across the aisle to where the men sat, Faith caught Adrian's eye. He didn't smile, but he gave a slight nod to acknowledge her. He'd overheard her conversation with Mrs. Zook, and Faith had the feeling he approved. A moment later, Anna asked Faith a question, forcing her to look away from Adrian.

As everyone waited for the *Vorsinger* to begin leading the first hymn, Faith closed her eyes. This was a solemn time, a time to prepare her heart and soul to rejoice and give thanks to the living God. She listened intently, willing her soul to open to God's presence, preparing to hear His word.

She heard the rustle of fabric on wooden benches as people shifted on the hard seats. In the trees outside, birds sang cheerfully, as if praising the Lord with their own special voices. In the barn below, Faith heard the movement of horses and cattle in their stalls. The smell of alfalfa hay and barn dust filled the air. She drew a deep breath. Contentment filled her bones. This was where she wanted to be. This was where she had always belonged.

She remembered how nervous she'd been the morning she took her vows. At nineteen, she had been the youngest of the group preparing for baptism. In that final hour before the service, she had searched her heart, wondering if she was making the right decision. It was no easy thing to live Amish.

She knew she had made the right choice.

The song leader, a young man with a red beard, started the first hymn. More than a hundred voices took up the solemn, slow-paced cadence. There was no music, only the stirring sounds of many voices praising God. Two ministers, a deacon and the bishop took their places on benches facing the congregation.

When the first song ended, the congregation sat in silence waiting for the preaching to begin. For Faith, it was a joyful moment. This was her first service in her new district and it felt as if she had come home at last.

Adrian did his best to listen to the sermon being preached, but his eyes were drawn constantly to where Faith sat. At the moment, her eyes were closed. There was such a look of peace on her face that he envied her.

He had not known peace or comfort during services since his son was killed. As hard as he tried to find consolation in the words being spoken, all he felt was anger.

Anger at God for robbing him of those most precious to him.

If he had his way, he would have stopped coming to church, but to do so would only bring more heartache to his family. If he avoided services, he would soon find himself under the ban, shunned by those who loved him in the hopes that he would mend his ways.

His brothers and sisters, his mother and father, none of them understood the anger that filled his heart, so he kept it hidden. He went through the motions of his faith without any substance. His life, which had once been filled with daily prayers, was now filled with hollow silence. God knew Adrian Lapp had not forgiven Him.

Adrian glanced at Faith. Was she even better at pretending faith than he was, or had she discovered the secret of letting go of her anger and hurt?

Beside him Benjamin fidgeted. His brother was eager to see the preaching end so he could visit with the Stultz sisters. The pretty twins were nearly the same age as Adrian's little brother. They were always willing to share their sweet smiles and laughter with him. Benjamin would soon be of courting age.

Adrian no longer believed in asking God for favors, but he hoped Benjamin would be spared the kind of pain he had endured, if and when Ben chose a wife.

Three hours later, when the service came to an end, Benjamin practically leaped from his seat and rushed to join his friends outside. Adrian stayed behind to help convert the benches into tables for eating by stacking them together. As he worked, he visited with his friends and neighbors. He listened to his father catching up on who had a sick horse, how everyone's corn was doing and what they planned to sell or buy on market day.

As the groups moved out of the barn toward the house, Adrian kept an eye out for Faith. He wanted to see if she was fitting in with the women of the district. He'd seen how scared she was when she first arrived.

He'd offered his advice without thinking twice. It was strange how easily he read her face and demeanor. Stranger still was how often he found himself thinking about her. She was an unusual woman.

Since there wasn't enough room to feed everyone inside the house, the ordained and the eldest church members ate first at the tables set up for them inside. The rest of the congregation took turns getting their food and carrying it out to the barn.

When it was Adrian's turn, he saw Faith had joined Nettie, her daughters and several other women and was working alongside them in the kitchen.

He relaxed when he saw her at ease, visiting with Sarah and Katie Sutter, holding Katie's baby on one hip as easily as any seasoned mother. It was good to see her happy and smiling.

He caught Nettie Sutter's eye. She smiled and nodded once. She was a good woman. She would do everything in her power to see that the women of the community welcomed Faith.

Adrian glanced away and caught Sarah studying him. She looked from him to Faith and then back again. Her grin widened. She beckoned him over. He immediately took his plate and went outside.

He finished his meal and was taking his plate back to the house when he saw Faith deep in conversation with Bishop Zook over on the front porch of the *dawdy haus*. Joseph motioned to Adrian. This time he had no choice but to obey.

The bishop smiled a broad welcome. "Adrian, I have been filling Faith in on our *ordnung*. I suggested she refer to you if she has any doubts about changes to her home or business as you are closer than I."

Faith remained silent, but a rosy blush stained her cheeks.

"I will do what I can to help." He didn't need a new excuse to see Faith, but he accepted the responsibility. It was important that she be accepted in the community. To do that, she had to live within the rules of their church.

The bishop thumped Adrian on the back. "Bless you. I knew I could count on you. A few of the men are getting up a game of quoits. Will you join us?"

Similar to horseshoes but played with round metal rings, quoits was a game Adrian used to enjoy, but he rarely took part in such activities now. "I will go find Ben. He has the best aim in the family."

After passing the message to his brother, Adrian put Ben in charge of getting the family home. With his duty discharged, Adrian left early and walked the few miles back to his farm.

At the house, he took a sharp knife and cut two bunches of flowers from the garden. With a bouquet in each hand, he walked out to the small cemetery where Gideon and Lovina waited for him.

Kneeling between their graves, he placed his gift beneath each headstone. "I brought some daisies for you, Lovey. I remember how much you loved them. You always said they were the bright eyes of your flowerbeds. They've bloomed all summer for you."

He sat back on his heels. "We held church services at Eli Imhoff's place. That *Englisch* fellow is still attending. I didn't think Jonathan would stay but he has a plain way about him now. Our new neighbor was there, too."

Pausing, he considered what to say about Faith. "She smoothed things over with Esther Zook right nicely. Course, I gave her a hint on how to handle Esther. I hope that's okay. She's a smart one, that Faith is."

Suddenly, it didn't feel right to be talking to his wife about another woman. He rose and took his usual place on the cedar stump.

The silence pressed in on him. The wind tugged at his hat, and he settled it more firmly on his head.

"Gideon, you should see the crazy animals that live next door to us now. Alpacas. They're cute, but they spit on people and each other if they get annoyed. Faith has ten of them. The yarn she spins from their fleece is mighty soft. She gave me a pair of socks. The ones I'm wearing now, in fact."

He pulled up his pant leg and fingered the material. The warm softness reminded him of Faith's smile when he'd caught her humming as she worked her spinning wheel on her front porch.

Pushing thoughts of her out of his head, he said, "I'm glad I'm not the fella who has to shear those beasties come spring. I'll bet he gets spit on a lot."

Adrian chuckled as he imagined anyone trying to clip the wool from Myrtle's neck.

The wind carried his mirth away. There was no answering laughter here. No one to share the joke with. Only two gray headstones among many in a field of green grass. Sadness settled in his chest, making it hard to breathe.

Adrian rose to his feet, shoved his hands in his pockets and started for home. It wasn't until he reached his lane that he realized he hadn't said goodbye.

On Monday afternoon Faith walked to the end of her lane and crossed the highway to the community phone. A small gray building not much bigger than a closet sat back from the road near a cluster of trees. A solar panel extended out from the south side of the roof. She could see through the window that it was unoccupied. She opened the door and stepped inside.

The shack held a phone, a small stool and a ledge for writing materials along with an answering machine blinking with two messages. She listened to them in case the agency had left a message for her, but they hadn't. Adrian had a message that his mower part was in, and Samuel Stultz had a new grand-baby over in Sugarcreek. It was a girl.

A local phone directory hung from a small chain at the side of the ledge. Picking it up, she searched for and found the number for the medical clinic in Hope Springs. She pulled a pencil and a piece of paper from her pocket to make note of the number for later. As she laid her pencil down, it rolled off the ledge and fell under her stool.

In the cramped space she couldn't reach it. She blew out her breath in a huff of disgust, then awkwardly squatted down, bracing herself against the door. A second later the door opened and she tumbled out backward, landing in a heap at Adrian Lapp's feet.

"Faith, are you all right?" He immediately dropped to one knee beside her.

She looked up into his face filled with concern and could have died of embarrassment. "I'm fine, but my dignity is a little bruised."

He helped her to her feet. "I'm sorry. I didn't see you. What were you doing on the floor?"

His hands lingered on her arms. She could feel the warmth and strength of them through the thin fabric of her dress. He was so close. His masculine scent enveloped her, sending a wave of heat rushing to her face that had nothing to do with embarrassment or fear. She wasn't frightened of him. His touch was strong but gentle. She was frightened by how much she wanted to move closer, to step into the circle of his arms and rest there.

She took a step back. He slowly let her go, his hands slip-ping from her elbows to her wrists in a soft caress. She said, "I dropped my pencil."

"What?" He seemed as confused as she was by the tension that shimmered between them.

"I was trying to reach my pencil. I dropped it and it rolled under the chair." She brushed at the back of her dress. Her blood hummed from his nearness and the way his gaze lingered on her face. Suddenly, she saw an attractive man in the prime of his life. A single man.

She crossed her arms and looked down, hoping he wouldn't read this new and disturbing awareness in her eyes.

"No wonder I didn't see you." He stepped inside the building and retrieved her pencil.

He held it out and she took it gingerly, careful not to touch him. *"Danki."*

"I will let you finish your call."

"I'm only making a doctor's appointment. If you need the phone, you may use it now. I can wait."

His brow furrowed into sharp lines. "Are you sick?"

She was flattered by the concern etched on his face. *"Nee,* it is nothing like that. The adoption agency I'm using requires me to have a physical. I need to have a fire safety inspection of my home, too. Do you have any idea who I would call to see about that?"

"Michael Klein is our local fire chief. I'm one of the volunteer firemen. His number is in the book."

"Michael Klein. I will remember that. What would I do without you, Adrian? You have helped me at every turn."

"I have no doubt you would manage. Make your calls. I can wait."

He walked away to stand in the shade, giving her some privacy. She went back inside the phone booth, quickly placed her first call and was happy to find out the doctor's office could see her that afternoon.

The second call went smoothly, as well. The fire chief agreed to come by the following day and inspect her home. With her appointments made, she stepped outside. "I'm finished, Adrian."

He walked over, but instead of taking a seat inside the phone booth, he leaned against the doorjamb. "How is your adoption going?"

Faith struggled against the urge to linger here with Adrian and lost. She liked his company; she liked spending time with him.

"Things are going well, I think. The doctor can see me today and the fire chief can come tomorrow. The social worker did not run screaming from my house, although when we were in the cellar, I thought she might."

"You have not introduced her to Myrtle, have you?" There was a glint of humor in his eyes and in his voice.

Faith grinned. "*Nee,* I made sure Miss Watkins stayed away from her."

"That's *goot.* The bishop's wife and I are forgiving of such an insult, but an *Englisch* woman in her fancy suit might not be."

The clip-clop of a horse and buggy approaching made them look toward the highway. Samuel Stultz pulled to a stop. "Are you using the phone?"

Faith grinned for she already knew his good news. "You have a message, Samuel."

As he hurried to get down, Faith turned to Adrian. "I must be going. I will have to hurry if I am to find the clinic in time for my appointment. Poor old Copper isn't as fast as she once was."

"I need to take a harness into Rueben Beachy's shop for repairs. I go right by the clinic if you want to ride with me."

"That is very kind of you, but I have no idea how long I will be."

They moved aside to let Samuel use the booth.

Adrian said, "I have several other errands to run. I need to pick up some bushel baskets and the new blades for my sickle mower should be in."

"They are. I heard it on the message machine." She leaned closer. "And Samuel has a new grandbaby."

Adrian chuckled, "I'm glad my blades have come in. It will be time to put up hay in another few days and I must be ready."

"Is the work in my orchard taking up too much of your time?"

"*Nee,* I'm glad of the extra work. I don't mind waiting for you at the doctor's office as long as you don't mind waiting there if you are done ahead of me."

A ride into town seated beside Adrian was more appealing than it should have been. Should she accept? What was the harm in it? There was no need for both their horses to make the trip. "I accept your offer, gladly, and I won't mind waiting."

"*Goot.* I will be back with my wagon in half an hour."

"I will be ready."

Samuel stuck his head out the door, a wide grin on his face. "I have a granddaughter."

Faith laughed. "I know. Congratulations."

When she looked back, Adrian had already started toward his farm. Faith bid Samuel good day and hurried as fast as she could to her house.

Once there, she quickly freshened up. She changed her worn and stained everyday dress and apron for her best outfit. After patting down a few stray hairs, she decided she looked well enough to go into town. The blue of her good dress brought out the color of her eyes. Would Adrian notice? The thought brought her up short. Now, she was being foolish.

Her practical nature quickly reasserted itself. It wasn't that she wanted to impress Adrian. She merely wanted to look presentable when she met the doctor. Having rationalized choosing her best dress, she gave one last look in the mirror, pinched some color into her cheeks, put on her bonnet and went out to wait for Adrian with excitement simmering in her blood.

Chapter Eight

Adrian called himself every kind of fool as he drove his green farm wagon up to Faith's gate. He was about to give his nosy neighbors and his family food for speculation by driving the widow Martin into town. Knowing smiles and pointed questions would be coming his way for days. What had he been thinking?

Cousin Sarah would be sure to hear about this. She would make certain his mother knew before the day was out. He began lining up explanations in his head so he would have them ready. His mother was certain to drop by his house before nightfall.

He tugged at his beard as the source of his coming discomfort limped down the walk and crossed behind the wagon to the passenger's side. He glanced down at her as she prepared to step up into the wagon. Something of what he'd been thinking must have shown on his face.

A look of concern furrowed her brow. "Is something wrong?"

There was no point in ruining her afternoon with his glum thoughts. He extended his hand to help her in. "*Nee*. I've much on my mind. That's all."

She laid her hand in his without hesitation. He realized it

was the first time she hadn't flinched away from him. A sense of satisfaction settled in the center of his chest.

Her hand was small and delicate in his grasp. His fist completely engulfed it. She was light as a feather when he pulled her up. She might be a tiny thing, but what she lacked in size she more than made up for in determination. He admired her tenacity. She had done a lot with her rundown inheritance. She was making the place into a home.

He turned the wagon around in the yard and set his gelding to a steady trot when they reached the highway. The drone of the tires on the payment, the clatter of the horse's hooves and the jangle of the harness were the only sounds for the first few minutes of the ride.

Adrian suddenly found himself tongue-tied. He hadn't spent time alone with a woman since his single days. What should he talk about? Or should he keep his mouth shut?

He glanced at Faith sitting straight as a board on the seat beside him. The wide brim of her black bonnet hid her face from his view. What was she thinking? Did she regret accepting his offer? Was she worried that gossips might link their names?

She spoke at last. "What is your horse called?"

"Wilbur."

"He has a fine gait."

Wilbur was a safe enough topic. "He was a racehorse in his younger days, but he was injured. His *Englisch* owner didn't want to waste money caring for him. You met Jonathan Dressler, didn't you?"

"The *Englisch* fellow who has become Amish?"

"*Ja*. He works for a group that takes in abandoned and injured horses. He nurses them back to health and retrains them for riding or buggy work."

"I'll remember that. My Copper is getting old and slowing down. I will need a new horse in a few years."

"Perhaps you can teach your alpacas to pull your buggy."

She giggled and shot a grin his way. "Can you see how many tourists would want my picture if I did such a thing?"

"Not many once they met Myrtle."

Faith laughed outright. His discomfort evaporated as warmth spread though his body. She had a way of making him forget his troubles. He said, "You should laugh more often."

Their eyes met, and she quickly looked away. "How soon will our peaches be ripe?"

"Another two or three weeks."

"Will you sell them from a roadside stand or take them into the market in town?"

"To market unless you want to run the stand?"

"I've been thinking about it. Do we get enough traffic on this road to make it worthwhile?"

Adrian relaxed and started to enjoy the ride as Faith asked about his plans for the orchard. A few pointed questions from him set her to talking about her alpacas and her plans for expanding her spinning business. It wasn't long before the town of Hope Springs came into view. As far as Adrian was concerned, the ride was over all too soon.

He left her at the door to the medical clinic and quickly set about completing his own errands so she wouldn't have to wait when she was done seeing the doctor. With a jolt, he realized he was eager for the trip home.

Faith entered the Hope Springs Clinic, a modern one-story blond brick building, with a sense of dread. She had spent more than enough time in hospitals and doctors' offices over the past two years. What if they found something new wrong with her? What if they thought she wasn't strong enough to take care of a child?

Inside the building, she checked in with the elderly receptionist and took a seat in the crowded waiting room. When her name was called, she followed a young woman in a white lab coat down a short hallway and took a seat on the exam room table.

The young woman introduced herself. "I'm Amber Bradley. I'm Dr. White's office nurse and a nurse-midwife. Can you tell me what kind of problems you've been having?"

"None." Faith withdrew her papers from her bag. "I am adopting a child, but first, I must have a physical."

Amber's smile widened as she took the paperwork. "Congratulations. The doctor will be with you in a few minutes. We will need to get any previous medical records you have. I'll bring you the forms to sign so we can get them faxed to this office."

"I'm very healthy. I did not see a doctor until I was in an accident two years ago." Faith opened her mouth for the thermometer Amber extended.

"That doesn't surprise me. Many Amish go their entire lives without seeing a doctor. We see a fair number here because of Dr. White's reasonable rates. I tell him he's just plain cheap." Amber chuckled as she recorded the temperature reading, then wrapped a blood pressure cuff around Faith's arm.

The outside door opened, and a tall, silver-haired man walked in. "Good afternoon, Mrs. Martin. I'm Dr. Harold White. What can we do for you today?"

Faith again explained her situation. The doctor listened carefully, then took the forms from Amber. "This looks pretty straightforward. We'll get a chest X-ray, draw some blood and give you a complete physical while you are here today. My office will send you the results in a few days. Do we have your address?"

Faith recited it, and the doctor wrote it down. He said, "Isn't this the old Delker Orchard?"

"*Ja.*"

Dr. White said, "That place has been empty for twenty years. I didn't know it was for sale."

"I inherited it when my husband passed away. He was the grandchild of the previous owner."

The doctor's eyebrows shot up. "He was that boy?"

Confused, Faith asked, "Did you know my husband?"

"I only met him once. I often wondered what happened to him. The whole thing was very hushed up at the time. Back then child abuse simply wasn't talked about."

Faith shook her head in denial. "You must be mistaken. He never spoke of such a thing."

"Was your husband's name Mose?"

"It was."

The doctor began counting to himself using his fingers, then said, "He would be forty-five years old if he were alive today."

She nodded. "He would."

"Did he have scars on both his wrists?"

"From where he was dragged by a runaway team of horses when he was small."

"I wish that were true. I'm not surprised he never spoke of it. Children who suffer such abuse often block it from their memory. His wrists were scarred from where he was tied up in his grandmother's basement. Apparently, he came to live with her when his parents both died of influenza. Old Mrs. Delker hated the Amish. Her only daughter ran away from home and wound up marrying an Amish fellow who left the faith for her."

"My husband said he was raised by his Amish grandparents after his parents passed away."

"Eventually, he was. I was called out to the farm when a utility worker reported he'd seen a boy chained in the cellar. The poor child was wearing only rags and he was thin as a rail. It was clear he'd been beaten and neglected. He hit and bit at anyone who came close to him."

Faith wrapped her arms around herself. "How terrible."

If only she had known. If only Mose had shared his pain instead of keeping it hidden all those years. Would their lives have been different? Surely they would have been.

Dr. White stared at the floor, as if watching that long-ago scene. "It was terrible. Eventually, the sheriff located his father's Amish parents and the boy was sent to live with them. Mrs. Delker spent some time in a mental hospital, but she came back within about six months. She was even more of a recluse afterwards. She had a stroke and passed away ten years later."

Dr. White looked up, suddenly contrite. "I'm so sorry. I shouldn't go on like that. Sometimes we old people don't know when to stop reminiscing. The past can seem clearer than the present for us. This must be quite a shock for you."

"It explains a lot about my husband. He wasn't a happy man."

"I'm sorry to hear that. Let us talk of more cheerful things. You are adopting a child. That's wonderful. The sooner we get done here, the sooner that can happen. The first thing we need from you is a medical history." He became all business.

Faith answered what seemed like a hundred questions, had her X-ray taken and suffered through getting her blood drawn, but the whole time she kept seeing Mose's face. He had been a harsh man without peace in his life. She prayed he was at peace now.

When she left the doctor's office, she saw Adrian waiting for her. The sight of him lifted her spirits.

"Are you finished?" he asked.

"*Ja.* And you?" She climbed up onto the wagon seat.

"All done. Shall we head home?"

"Would you mind if we stopped at the fabric store? I need

to see if I should bring in more yarn." She was in no hurry to return to the house that had seen such pain.

A fleeting look of reluctance flashed across Adrian's face. "*Ja,* we can stop at the fabric store."

"If it's too much trouble, I can wait," she offered, not wanting to upset him.

"It's no trouble at all," he drawled. Slapping the reins against Wilbur's rump, he set the black horse in motion.

When they reached Needles and Pins, Faith scrambled down from the bench seat. "I'll just be a minute."

A wry smile twisted his lips. "Take your time and say hello to Sarah for me. Tell her I'll be expecting *Mamm* this evening."

Faith wasn't quite sure what to make of his odd mood. He glanced toward the shop door as it opened and said, "Never mind. Here she comes now."

Faith turned around, expecting to see Sarah, but saw instead a short, gray-haired woman coming out of the shop. She stopped abruptly when she caught sight of Adrian, then smiled broadly.

"Hello, my son. What are you doing here?"

"I had some errands to run. *Mamm,* have you met Faith Martin?"

"I have not." His mother subjected Faith to intense scrutiny.

Faith was glad she'd taken the time to change her dress and put on her best bonnet. "I'm pleased to meet you, Mrs. Lapp. Your son has been wonderfully helpful to me. He has been the best neighbor anyone could ask for."

"Please call me Linda. It does a mother's heart good to hear such things about her son. I saw you briefly at the last church service, but I failed to introduce myself. I've been remiss in not welcoming you. Please forgive me."

"There is nothing to forgive. Excuse me, I must check

to see if Janet needs more yarn from me. I won't be long, Adrian."

"No hurry," he replied.

Linda's grin widened. There was a distinctive twinkle in her eyes. "Your papa and I must stop by for a visit one of these evenings, Adrian. We have some catching up to do."

He knew where she was going and sought to cut her off. "Don't read more into this than there is. I'm helping out a neighbor. That's all."

Her smile faded. "It's time you put your grief away and took a close look at your life, my son. Many wonders of God are missed by a man who will not open his eyes."

As his mother walked away, Adrian mulled her words. How did he put away his grief even if he wanted to? Did he want to?

His grief had become a high fence he used to hold others at bay. In spite of his efforts, and without meaning to, Faith Martin had made a hole in that fence. To close it back up meant pushing her out of his life. Was he willing to do that?

Even if he wanted to, he wasn't sure he could. There was something special about her, something more than her pretty face and expressive eyes. When he was with her…he felt alive for the first time in years.

True to her word, Faith was back in a few minutes. He glanced at her seated beside him as they rode homeward. She was unusually quiet. Her eyes held a faraway look, as if she were viewing something sad from her past.

Was she remembering trips she'd taken with her husband seated beside her? Had the doctor given her bad news? Did her leg hurt? Was she tired?

There were so many things he wanted to know about her, so many questions he wanted to ask, but he shied away from them because they might reveal the real question nagging at the back of his mind.

Did Faith enjoy being in his company as much as he enjoyed being with her?

The afternoon sun beat down on them as they traveled along. Faith untied her dark bonnet and laid it on the seat between them. He asked, "Are you warm?"

"A little."

Stupid question. Of course she was or she wouldn't have taken off her bonnet. Why did he revert to acting like a tongue-tied teenager around this woman?

They made the rest of the journey to her home in silence. When he pulled to a stop in front of her gate, she didn't get down but sat staring at the house like she'd never seen it before. She asked, "Did you know the woman who lived here before I came?"

"Vaguely."

"Was she evil?"

What a strange question. "I don't think so. She was old, and *ab im kopp.*"

"Off in the head? Crazy?"

"Ja."

"She must have been," Faith whispered.

He covered her hand with his. "Is something wrong?"

She didn't look at him. Her eyes remained fixed on the house. He checked out the building but didn't see anything amiss. What was going on?

Gazing back at Faith, he studied her face intently. It was as if she couldn't see or hear him. He squeezed her fingers. "Faith, what's the matter?"

Her gaze slid to their hands and then to his face. She pulled away sharply and climbed down from the wagon, mumbling, "Goodbye."

Stunned by her abrupt departure, Adrian stared after her. Had he done something wrong? Had he upset her with something he said? Should he follow her and ask or leave her be?

The safe thing to do was to leave her be. He was becoming far too caught up in Faith Martin's life. He'd been neglecting his own work to help her, something he never did. This had to stop.

He turned the wagon and started for home. He'd only gone a hundred yards when he noticed her bonnet on the seat beside him.

Stopping the horse, he picked up the bonnet and held it in his hands. The dark fabric was warm from the sun. He lifted it to his face and breathed in. It held her scent.

He looked over his shoulder toward her house. Perhaps he was too caught up in her life, but he was ready to admit he was deeply drawn to Faith. He saw no way to free himself unless she turned him away.

Looping the reins over the brake handle, he jumped down from the wagon and strode toward her gate not knowing if he was simply returning her belonging or starting down a whole new path in his life.

When he reached the porch, he saw the front door stood open. He climbed the steps and called her name. She didn't answer. Pausing in the doorway, he started to call out again when a sound stopped him. Someone was crying.

"Faith?" He took a step inside. The muffled sounds of sobbing were coming from a doorway at the back of the kitchen. Hesitantly, he walked that way.

The second he realized the door led to the cellar, he rushed forward. Had she fallen? Was she injured? "Faith, is that you? Are you all right?"

It took a second for his eyes to adjust to the darkness below him. When they did, he could just make out her form at the bottom of the stairs. She sat huddled into a ball on the bottom riser with her arms around her knees. Her shoulders shook with sobs.

He descended quickly, stepping past her to crouch in front

of her. He laid his hand gently on her shoulder. "Faith, did you fall? Are you hurt?"

She lifted her head and shook it in denial as she wiped the tears from her cheeks.

His heart began beating again with rapid erratic thuds. "You scared the life out of me. What's wrong?"

Words began pouring out of her. "If only I had known, I would have been a better wife. How could he keep such a thing locked away from me?"

"Faith, I don't understand."

"I married Mose because my parents were gone, my brother had left the faith and I had no one. I didn't love him as a wife should. I tried, but I couldn't, and I'm so ashamed." She buried her face in her hands.

This was way out of his depths. Faith needed another woman to talk to. Someone like his mother or Nettie, but he couldn't leave her weeping in the cellar.

No, that wasn't true. He could leave, but he didn't want to.

Adrian settled himself on the narrow step beside her. His hip brushed against hers. Her shoulder, where it touched his, spread warmth all down his arm. He wanted nothing more than to slip his arm around her and comfort her, but he knew it wouldn't be right. Such closeness between a man and a woman was for husbands and wives.

He had no idea what to say. He simply started talking. "I loved my wife dearly, but I can't remember her face. I try so hard to see her, but she isn't clear anymore. I'm ashamed of that. How can I forget the one I loved more than my own life?"

Faith sniffed and slanted a look his way. "You should not feel ashamed for that."

"Nor should you feel shame. We are only human."

Nodding, she looked away from him, staring into the dark

corner of the room. "My husband was a cruel man. I think he tried not to be, but he couldn't help himself. I used to think it was my fault. I thought I couldn't make him happy because I didn't love him enough."

Adrian's breath froze in his chest. "He was cruel to you?"

She looked down at her hands and gave a tiny nod.

Was she saying what he thought she was saying? "Faith, did your husband beat you?"

She nodded again, as if words were beyond her.

His stomach contracted with disgust. No wonder she flinched from his touch. What kind of man could abuse someone as sweet and kind as Faith?

"No man has the right to be cruel to another in such a fashion. It was not your fault."

Scrubbing her face with her hands, she said, "I know."

She drew a deep breath and looked at Adrian. "My husband's grandmother lived here. Her daughter ran away with an Amish lad. When they died, Mose came back to stay with her."

"Are you sure? I don't remember a boy living here."

"Mose was twelve years older than I. You wouldn't have been old enough to know him, but, in truth, no one knew he was here. His grandmother kept him locked away in this cellar until the sheriff learned of it and took him away. Dr. White told me the whole sad story today."

"That's why you were so quiet on the way home."

"I kept thinking that I was the one person who should have loved him and I didn't. If I had, he might have shared this pain with me and been healed."

"You take too much onto yourself. Only God can know the hearts and minds of men. You would have helped your husband if you could. You have a kind heart, Faith Martin."

She shook her head in denial. "You are the one with the kind heart."

He gently cupped her face and turned it toward him. With the pad of his thumb, he brushed the tears from her cheeks. Her luminous, tear-filled eyes widened, and her lips parted.

She was so close, so warm, so vibrant, and yet so vulnerable. He could kiss her—wanted to kiss her. He wanted to taste the sweetness of her soft lips, but something held him back.

Faith needed a friend now, not another complication. If he gave in to his desire it would change everything between them. She had given him a rare gift. Her trust. He didn't want to do anything to jeopardize that.

Faith closed her eyes and leaned into Adrian's hand, drawing strength from his gentle touch. If only she could hold on to this moment forever. She'd never felt so safe.

Why did this man make her wish for things that could never be? Long ago she'd given up the notion of having a happy marriage and children of her own. That wasn't God's plan for her. She accepted that.

And now this man had come into her life. A kind, sweet man who made her wish she still believed in a marriage with love between a husband and a wife. She cared for Adrian. Deeply.

As much as she wanted to hold on to this moment, she couldn't. She couldn't allow her growing feelings for Adrian to distract her. She had to think about Kyle. She had to focus on his adoption and on providing him with a safe, secure home.

She pulled away from Adrian. He withdrew his hand. The coolness of the cellar air made her shiver.

Pity filled his voice as he said, "Come upstairs, Faith. You cannot change what happened here. It is all in God's hands now."

Pity for her or for her husband?

She'd shared her darkest secret with Adrian. Did he think less of her for suffering in silence all those many years? Maybe she didn't want to know.

She struggled to her feet. "I didn't mean to burden you with my woes."

"They are no burden, Faith. Sharing your troubles makes them lighter."

She realized he was right. Her unhappy past didn't loom over her the way it once had. Her sense of relief left her light-headed. She started up the stairs. "You have work to do. You should go home."

"There's nothing that can't wait. Are you sure you're okay?"

"*Ja,* a stout cup of tea will fix me right up." She entered the kitchen and crossed to the sink. Her hands trembled as she reached for the teakettle. The room began spinning around her.

Adrian was beside her in an instant. His hand closed over hers as he gently took the kettle from her. "Let me do this. You sit down."

He took her by the elbow and led her to the table. Pulling out a chair, he held it while she sat, then he returned to the sink and began to fill the kettle.

She drew several deep breaths. "Adrian, you don't have to take care of me."

"If I don't, who will?" He carried the kettle to the stove. He turned on the burners and set the kettle over the flames, then started opening cabinets. "Where do you keep your tea?"

"In the green tin on the counter beside the refrigerator."

He found it and soon had a mug ready for the hot water. As he waited for the kettle to boil, he took a seat across the table from her.

She managed a small smile. "God is *goot* to give me

a friend such as you. Are you so thoughtful of all your neighbors?"

"Only the ones with animals that spit on me."

She chuckled. "Poor man. What an impression we must have made on you. It's a wonder you ever came back."

"I reckon I came back because I didn't think you could make a go of this place. You proved me wrong."

Lacing her fingers together in front of her on the table, she said, "I've managed to hang on for a few weeks. That doesn't mean I can hang on forever. It doesn't mean the *Englisch* will think this is a good home for my nephew."

"What will happen if they don't let you adopt him?"

Faith closed her eyes. "I can't think such a thing. They *must* let him stay with me. I don't think I could bear it if they don't."

Adrian laid his hand over her clenched fingers. She opened her eyes to find him gazing at her with compassion and something else in his eyes. Longing.

Her heart began beating faster. He started to speak, but the shrill whistle of the kettle cut him off.

He pulled his hand away and rose to fix her tea. Whatever he had been about to say remained unsaid. After bringing her mug to the table, he muttered a goodbye and left abruptly. As the screen door banged shut behind him, Faith was left to wonder if she had imagined the closeness they had shared so briefly.

Chapter Nine

Two days after taking Faith into town, Adrian was cutting hay in the meadow when a car turned in his lane. It stopped on the road not far from him, and an *Englisch* lady got out. He drew his team to a halt. She approached but kept a wary eye on his horses. "Are you Mr. Adrian Lapp?"

"I am." He waited for her to state her business.

"I'm Caroline Watkins. I'm the social worker in charge of your neighbor's adoption application. I've just come from my second visit here, and Mrs. Martin has given me permission to speak with some of her neighbors. May I have a few minutes of your time?"

He wiped the sweat from his brow with his shirtsleeve and adjusted his hat. "A few. I must get my hay cut."

"I won't take long, I promise." She opened a leather folder and began to write in it.

Meg, the horse closest to her, stomped at a fly and shook her head. Miss Watkins stumbled back a step and looked ready to run to the safety of her car. Time was a wasting. Adrian said, "What questions have you?"

She gave an embarrassed smile but didn't come closer. "How long have you known Faith Martin?"

"Three weeks, I reckon."

"Is that all?"

"I met her the day after she arrived here."

Miss Watkins kept writing. "Are you aware of any reason why Mrs. Martin should not adopt a child?"

"Nee."

"Do you believe she can provide for a child?"

"I do, but it makes no difference if she can or not."

Miss Watkins's brows drew together in a frown. "Of course it makes a difference."

"An Amish parent does not need to worry about what will happen to his or her family if something tragic befalls them. All our widows and children are well cared for."

"By whom?"

It was clear this outsider didn't understand Amish ways. "Our church members will see that Faith and her child have food, clothing and a roof over their heads if ever they need such help."

"That's very admirable."

"It is the way God commands us to live."

"Have you seen Mrs. Martin interacting with children?"

He thought back to last Sunday. *"Ja."*

"Tell me about it."

"I saw her holding Katie Sutter's daughter, Rachel. She had the babe settled on her hip. It looked as if she had done it many times. I also saw her with Annie Imhoff. She is nine, I think. Faith gave her attention and directed her to help with the work as was right."

"What are your feelings about Faith's adoption plan?"

"It is a *goot* thing for her to take in her brother's child, or any child."

"How often do you see Mrs. Martin?"

"I've seen her almost daily since she arrived."

"And why is that?"

The question shocked him. Why had he found excuse after excuse to trek across the field to see her so often?

Wasn't it because he was happier when he was near her? Wasn't it because her smile drove away his loneliness?

Miss Watkins waited for his reply. He said, "Because she needs help and it is the neighborly thing to do."

"Describe her personal qualities and limitations."

At last an easy question. "She is hardworking. She is devout. Modest. She is kind to her animals."

Miss Watkins stopped writing and looked up. "And what about her limitations?"

A not-so-easy question. What could he say that wouldn't undermine her chances of adopting her nephew and yet was the truth? "She sometimes takes on more than she can handle."

"Do you see her physical handicap as a limitation?"

"You and I might see it as such, but she does not," he stated firmly.

"Can you describe her potential ability to parent?"

"She will make a fine mother." Of that he had no doubt.

Miss Watkins folded her notebook tight against her chest. "Will a child of a different faith be accepted in your community?"

He shouldn't be annoyed by her ignorance, but he was. "God loves all His children. How could we do any less? Faith's nephew will be raised to know and serve God, as all our children are. To become Amish is a choice, not a requirement. When he is old enough, he will make that decision for himself. I must get back to work now."

"Thank you for your time."

He clicked his tongue. "Get up, Meg. Go along, Mick."

The team began moving and set the sickle in motion. The clatter of the razor sharp blades drowned out the sound of Miss Watkins' car as she drove away.

It wasn't right that an outsider was the one to decide if Faith could adopt her nephew.

For the first time in many years, Adrian opened his heart and prayed. He prayed for God to smile on Faith and the child who needed her.

In the middle of the week, Faith purchased a used woodstove at a farm sale and had it installed in her home. She bid a sad goodbye to the propane stove but happily pocketed the money from its sale. Her first attempt to use her new stove resulted in a charred meal, but by the third day she had the hang of it again.

The fire chief's favorable inspection report arrived in the mail a week later, the same day her medical report came. Dr. White had found her in sound health. She mailed the reports along with mounds of paperwork to the adoption agency and waited for a reply.

The following week she opened her mail to find the news she had been waiting for.

Kyle was coming to stay with her...on a trial basis.

Finally!

Faith hugged the letter to her chest and twirled in a circle, nearly falling in the process.

When she was calm enough, she read the details again. There would be more follow-up visits by the agency after Kyle arrived, but if all went well, the adoption hearing was scheduled for the last Monday in September.

There could still be stumbling blocks, but Faith didn't care. Kyle was on his way. She was finally going to meet her brother's child.

As she waited impatiently on the porch the day he was to arrive, she worked at carding her fleece. The process of combing sections of hair over and over again between two brushes was a mindless task she could do as she watched the driveway. Each passing minute felt like an hour.

When Miss Watkins's car finally appeared, Faith dropped her work into a basket and walked toward her gate, her hands shaking with excitement. She had waited so long for this moment.

Caroline stopped her car and got out. Without a word, she opened the back door of the automobile. Faith smiled happily at the boy who emerged. With his flaming red hair and freckles, young Kyle was the spitting image of his father at the same age.

The anxiety Faith had been living with for weeks lifted away and vanished into the air like smoke. It took but a moment for love to form in her heart. This was her brother's son, and she would love him as she had his father. As she would love her own child.

"Welcome, Kyle. I am your *Aenti* Faith, and I am very pleased to meet you."

He looked ready to bolt back into the car. His green eyes held sadness and fear. The tragedy had left its mark on him. Faith could have wept for all he had endured. It would be up to her and God to see that Kyle's life was safe and happy from now on out.

Miss Watkins said, "Today is a very special day. It's Kyle's birthday. I didn't know if you knew that or not."

Faith grinned at Kyle. "I didn't know. Happy birthday, dearest. My goodness, you are six. We will have to get you enrolled in school right away if you are to start this fall."

She took a step closer and bent to his level. "I have a surprise for you. Someone else has arrived just this morning and I think he would like to meet you."

Kyle's gaze moved from her face to the house behind her. "Who is it?"

Faith straightened and crossed her arms. "Well, I don't

know what to call him. He's down in the barn. Would you like to meet him?"

Kyle eyed the barn with uncertainty. "I guess."

"*Goot.* Come along. Miss Watkins, you are welcome to come, too." Faith nodded in that direction.

The social worker looked from the barn down to her high-heeled shoes. "I believe I'll wait in the house."

Faith extended her hand to Kyle but he didn't take it. She tried not to feel rejected. She knew she needed to give him time to warm up to her. She started toward the barn and glanced over her shoulder. Kyle followed.

Happiness warmed her heart. It had been a long time since she'd dared believe she could be this happy.

At the barn door, she waited for him to catch up. "Have you ever been to a farm before?"

He hooked his thumbs in the waistband of his jeans. "We stayed on a ranch once. The rancher was a friend of my mom's. They had a whole lotta cows and cowboys, too."

Faith smiled at his southern drawl. He had lived his whole life in Texas and it showed.

She opened the door. "I don't have a cow yet, but we will have to get one soon so you can have fresh milk to drink. There are lots of things you will learn about living on a farm, but one of the most important things is to respect the animals."

A loud whinny came from inside. Kyle's eyes grew round. "You've got a horse?"

She grinned at the excitement in his voice. "It is your horse now, too."

"Can I see him?" His wariness gave way to tempered eagerness.

"It's a she. Our mare's name is Copper. You can see her in a minute. A horse is a very strong animal and can hurt you if you aren't careful. I want you to listen carefully to these two rules. Are you listening?"

He nodded.

"Never run behind a horse. Never. Always speak to them softly so that they know where you are. Can your repeat these rules for me?"

"I never run behind one and I speak softly so they know I'm there."

"That's right. Okay, come and meet Copper." Faith led the way down the narrow center aisle to the first stall on the right. Copper hung her head over the boards to investigate the newcomer.

Kyle took a step closer to Faith. "She's really big."

"Wait until you see my neighbor's draft horses. They are really, really big. They make poor Copper look like a pony beside them."

Kyle started to hold out his hand but snatched it back when Copper nibbled at it. "Does she bite?"

"She is looking for a treat. I just happen to have something she loves in my pocket. I will show you how to feed her."

Faith withdrew a kerchief from her pocket and opened it to reveal several apple slices. Taking one, she laid it in the center of Kyle's palm. "Keep your hand flat. You don't want her to think your fingers are the treats."

He bravely held up the slice. Copper daintily nibbled it up. Kyle wiped his hand on his jeans. "Her lips are soft but her chin whiskers tickle. Can I give her another one?"

"Of course."

He fed her two more apple bits and then grew brave enough to pet her nose. "Can you teach me how to ride her?"

"I can, but Copper is a buggy horse."

"Like the ones I saw on the highway coming here?"

"*Ja,* just like those. Come, I have some more animals for

you to meet." She smiled at Kyle and wondered what Adrian would think of her *Englisch* nephew.

Leading the way to the back of the barn, Faith stopped beside the last stall. "This is who I want you to meet."

She pointed through the board to the farthest corner. Myrtle lay in the thick bed of hay Adrian had spread out for her. At her side, a coal-black cria lay beside her. He raised his long neck that still wobbled slightly and batted his thick eyelashes in their direction.

"Is that a camel?" Kyle climbed up the boards to get a better view. Faith was pleased to see his curiosity pushing aside his unease.

"It's an alpaca. Her name is Myrtle and that is her new son. He doesn't have a name yet. He was just born this morning."

"Sweet. Can I pet him?"

"As long as his mother doesn't object. Come, I will introduce you so that she knows you are a friend."

Faith opened the gate and stepped inside the pen. Her feet sank into the soft hay, making her stumble. Myrtle shot to her feet in alarm. The cria struggled to its feet and ducked under his mother's body to hide on the other side of her legs.

"What's the matter with your leg?" Kyle had noticed her brace.

"I hurt it a long time ago and it didn't heal well so now I have to wear this brace."

"Does it hurt?"

"Sometimes, but not today."

Grasping the gate to steady herself, Faith spoke soothingly to Myrtle in Pennsylvania Dutch. When the new mother was calm, Faith crossed the pen carefully with Kyle at her side. Myrtle allowed them both to admire her baby, but the baby remained hidden behind his mother.

Kyle squatted down in the bedding and held out his hand. "Come here, little fella. I won't hurt you."

"Perhaps he wants a name first. What do you think we should call him? He's black as night. Shall we call him Midnight?"

"No, that's a girly name."

Feeling put in her girly place, Faith held back a chuckle. "All right, what would you like to call him?"

"I want to call him Shadow."

She considered it. "Shadow. I think that's a very good name for him."

By this time the cria had grown accustomed to their presence and ventured out from behind his mother. Kyle extended his hand. "Come here, Shadow."

Shadow approached slowly, wobbling as he walked. Barely bigger than a tomcat with impossibly long legs, he was still trying to learn to use them.

It was clear he was as curious about the boy as the boy was about him. Kyle inched forward and touched the baby alpaca's head. Shadow frisked away behind his mother but didn't stay there. He returned after a moment to investigate further.

Faith said, "Kyle, I think he likes you."

"I think so, too."

"Since you have chosen his name, would you like to be his owner?"

"Can I?" Kyle looked up with uncertainty in his eyes.

"There are many things you will have to learn in order to take good care of him. It will be hard work. Are you willing to do that?"

"Sure."

"I don't mean for one day. I mean everyday."

"If you show me what to do."

Myrtle began stamping one foot and making huffing

sounds. Faith said, "His mother says he has had enough play time. We should let him rest."

"He's really neat. Thanks, Aunt Faith."

She held open the gate to let him out of the stall. "You're welcome, Kyle. Let's go back to the house. I'm sure Miss Watkins is wondering where we are."

When they reached the house, Kyle went in ahead of her. Miss Watkins sat at the kitchen table fanning herself with a sheet of paper. Faith said, "Kyle, why don't you go explore the house."

"Okay." He left the room.

Miss Watkins slid several sheets of paper toward Faith. "We have only two more documents to sign, Mrs. Martin. It won't take long. Now, you understand this is a temporary guardianship until the court hearing next month."

"*Ja,* I understand."

"Good. I'll be back to visit Kyle several times before the hearing and see how things are going for the two of you. Expect me at noon the day after tomorrow. These transitions don't always go smoothly, so be prepared for that."

"I will."

After Faith signed the papers waiting for her, she walked with Miss Watkins to the door. "Thank you for all your help."

"I'm just doing my job. The judge will consider my recommendations when making a decision about the adoption."

"Of course." Faith wanted to hug the woman. It was finally sinking in. Kyle was here. At long last, God had given her a child.

"Aunt Faith?"

She and Miss Watkins turned around. Faith asked, "What is it, Kyle?"

"Where's your TV?"

* * *

At the end of their first day together, Faith helped Kyle get ready for bed. The scared, lost look she'd seen on his face when he'd first arrived had returned.

Setting his suitcase on a chair beside the bed, she began putting his clothes into the lowest drawers of the dresser against the wall where small hands could reach them easily.

Her hand encountered something hard tucked in between his pajamas and T-shirts. When she pulled it out, she saw it was a photograph of her brother and his wife.

Faith let her hand drift over the glass as she studied her brother's face. He had changed a great deal in the twelve years that he'd been gone. A man looked back at her, not the boy she remembered. The woman with him had dark brown hair and green eyes, a stunning combination.

"That's my mom and dad." Kyle reached for the picture.

"You look just like him." She handed the forbidden image to the boy.

He kissed the picture and looked around the room. "I think I'll want this by the bed so I can see it when I open my eyes."

She didn't have the heart to tell him the photograph would have to be put away. He had lost too much already. She wouldn't take away this reminder of his parents. Not yet.

She patted his head. "On your bedside table will be fine for now."

Turning away, she opened his windows to dispel the room's stuffiness and to hide the tears that stung her eyes. When she had a grip on her raw emotions, she turned around. He was already under the covers.

"You will be too hot under all of this." She drew back the quilt and folded it to the foot of the bed, leaving him with just a sheet.

He looked around, then sat up in bed. "I need a fan to sleep with."

"I don't have one. The breeze from the windows will keep you cool."

He pointed at the lantern she had placed on the dresser. "Can I keep the light on?"

"If you leave it on all night the battery will go dead."

"Please? I don't like the dark."

"I reckon it'll be okay. I have more batteries."

Relief flickered in his eyes. He scooted down in bed and pulled the sheet up to his chin. His red hair and freckles stood out in stark relief against the white bedclothes. Once again she was reminded of his father.

She asked, "Do you want to say your prayers before you go to sleep?"

He pressed his lips together and shook his head. "I don't know any."

Surprised, she asked, "You don't? Did not your mother and father teach you your prayers?"

"I know one but I don't like it anymore."

"I'll tell you what. I will say my prayers and you can listen and add anything you want to say. How's that?"

He didn't consent, but he didn't object so Faith dropped awkwardly to her knees. Pain shot through her leg, but she ignored it. She folded her hands and bowed her head.

"Dear Father in heaven, Kyle and I give you thanks for the blessings You have shown us today. I'm so happy that he is here with me. Thank You for bringing him safely to my home."

"You could say thanks for giving me Shadow," Kyle whispered.

She nodded and closed her eyes. "Kyle and I both want to thank You for the gift of little Shadow. He brings us great joy with his playful ways."

She peeked at her nephew. "Anything else?"

He shook his head. Closing her eyes again, she said, "Bless us and help us to do Your will, Lord. Help us to live as You would have us live, humbly and simply, ever mindful of Your grace as we go about our daily tasks. Forgive us our sins as we forgive those who have sinned against us. Amen."

"Are you done?" he asked.

She smiled softly at him. "I'm done."

"Where are you going to sleep?" Worry crept back into his voice as she struggled to her feet.

Tucking the sheet around him, she said, "I will be right across the hall. If you need anything, just call out. Okay?"

"I guess. Can you leave the door open?"

"Certainly. Try to get some sleep."

"Am I going to stay here a long time?"

"I hope so, darling."

"Who decides if I stay or go to a another house? Do you?"

"It will be up to Miss Watkins and a judge to decide. If God wishes it, you will stay with me a long, long time." She bent down, kissed his brow and went to her own room.

Hours later she came awake with a jolt. Someone was screaming.

"Mommy! Mommy!"

Kyle! She shot out of bed, stumbling without her brace toward his room.

Chapter Ten

The door to Kyle's room stood open, but he wasn't in the bed. Frantic, Faith rushed in and searched the room. The lantern's battery was nearly depleted. It gave only a feeble, flickering light, but it was enough to let her see him huddled in the corner by the closet.

Some instinct made her approach him slowly. "Kyle, dearest, what's wrong?"

His eyes were open, but she knew he wasn't seeing her. He turned his head from side to side, sobbing. "Mommy? Mommy?"

Faith lowered herself to the floor. "Kyle, it's *Aenti* Faith. Can you hear me? Everything is all right. You've had a nightmare, that's all."

He sat with his arms around his knees. His little body trembled violently.

Faith moved closer. "It's all right, baby. It's all right. I'm here."

Suddenly, his eyes focused on her. He launched himself into her arms. Faith held him close, rocking him and stroking his hair as she murmured words of comfort.

He said, "I don't like it here. I want to go home."

"You are home, sweetheart. This is your new home, now."

He didn't answer, but slowly, his sobs died away. After a time, he fell asleep.

Faith sat holding him for a long time. Her heart bled for the pain he had endured in his young life. She could only pray that time and her love would heal his wounded soul.

When she was sure he was fast asleep, she struggled to her feet and carried him to his bed. After tucking him in, she lay down beside him in case he woke again and waited for the morning to come.

Miss Watkins would be back to check on him at noon tomorrow. If she learned how unhappy he was, would she take him away?

Late-morning sunshine glinted through the orchard canopy dappling the ground with dancing patterns of light and shadow as Adrian set to work harvesting the first of Faith's fruit. He hadn't been at it long when the hair at the back of his neck started to prickle.

Someone was watching him.

He lowered his fruit-picking pole to the ground. One of the alpacas, perhaps?

A quick check around showed he had Faith's orchard to himself. Shrugging off the feeling, he raised a long pole with a wire basket and a branch snipper on the end up into the branches of Faith's trees. As he worked, he transferred the peaches he'd plucked into a bushel basket at his feet. When he was finished gathering the fruit from one tree, he moved on to another. The feeling that he was being watched didn't leave.

As he emptied the pole basket into a larger one, a shower of leaves made him look up into the tree above him. The sight that greeted his eyes sent a slash of pain through his heart.

A red-haired, freckled-faced *kind* peered down through the leaves of a peach tree. The boy looked so much like his son that for a second he thought he was dreaming.

"Gideon?" He barely breathed the name.

The face disappeared back into the foliage. A small, disembodied voice asked, "Are you going to make me go away?"

The voice didn't belong to Gideon. This wasn't his son come back from the grave. Who was it? Adrian said, "Come down from there."

A few seconds later a pair of sneakers appeared. A boy lowered himself until he hung suspended from a branch with his shoes about three feet off the ground.

The kid shot Adrian a scowl. "Can I get a little help here?"

Adrian's racing heart slowed. Now that he had a better view of the boy, he could see the red hair and freckles were the only things that were similar to his son. This was an *Englisch* boy. He was several years older than Gideon had been. Stepping forward, Adrian grasped the boy's waist and lowered him to the ground.

"Thanks." The kid dusted his hands together, then cocked his head to the side as he studied Adrian. "Well?"

"Well what?"

"Are you going to take me away?"

"*Nee.*"

"Are you going to be my new dad if the judge makes Aunt Faith my new mom?"

Realization dawned on Adrian. The boy was Faith's nephew. He breathed a silent prayer of thanks that God had seen fit to bring her the child she longed for.

"I will not be your father. I'm a neighbor from down the road. I'm helping your *aenti* harvest her peaches."

"Oh. That's okay then. I didn't want a new dad. Aunt Faith

is nice and all, but I want my real dad and mom to come back."

"They cannot come back from heaven."

Looking down, the boy kicked a fallen peach and sent it rolling through the grass. "Yeah, I know."

Adrian knew exactly what the boy was feeling. He said, "My name is Adrian Lapp. What is yours?"

"Howdy, Mr. Lapp. I'm Kyle King," the boy drawled.

"If you have nothing better to do, Kyle King, you can help me finish picking this fruit."

He didn't look enthused. "I don't know how. Do you have TV at your house?"

"*Nee,* it is *veldlich* and is *verboten.*"

"Huh?"

"It is a worldly thing and forbidden to us."

"How come you talk so funny?"

"Because I am Amish. How come you talk so funny?"

Kyle's solemn face cracked a tiny smile. "Because I'm a Texan."

"Ah. Do they have peaches in Texas?"

"I guess."

"But you have never picked peaches in Texas."

"Nope. We lived in Houston. Mom got our peaches from the grocery store."

"Houston, is that a big town?"

Kyle raised one eyebrow. "Are you kidding me?"

"*Nee,* I am not."

"What does *nee* mean?"

"It is Pennsylvania Dutch and it means no."

"Then why don't you just say no?"

"Because I am Amish and that is the language we speak."

"Oh. My aunt Faith is Amish, too. That's why she wears those funny dresses and that thing on her head."

"It is called a prayer *kapp*. It signifies her devotion to God."

"I'm not going to wear one 'cause I don't like God. He's mean."

"You must not say such a thing."

"It's true. My foster mom said God wanted my mom and dad with Him in heaven more than He wanted them to be here. That proves He isn't nice."

"I think she meant God *needed* them in heaven more than He needed them here."

Those were the same words Adrian's family and friends had used to try and comfort him, to help explain the inexplicable reasons why first his wife and then his son had been taken away. Like Kyle, Adrian found no comfort in the words.

The boy picked up a peach and threw it against a nearby tree, splattering the soft fruit against the rough bark. "I needed them more."

Faced with the impotent fury of this child, Adrian put aside his own feelings of bitterness and sought a way to help the boy. "You have a good arm, Kyle. Do you like baseball?"

"Sure. My dad was the coach of my team. He taught me everything about baseball. He was going to get me a new mitt when he picked me up after school, but he never came back. Why did God have to take him away?"

Adrian plucked a wormy peach from an overhead branch and threw it. It smashed into bits against the same tree. "We cannot know God's reasons. We can only pray that one day we will see our loved ones again."

"Did your parents die, too?"

"No. God took my wife and my son to heaven."

Kyle chucked two peaches toward the hapless tree. Only one hit the target. He squinted up at Adrian. "So, do you hate God, too?"

* * *

Faith faced Miss Watkins across the kitchen table. This was the social worker's first visit to see how Kyle was adjusting to life on the farm. Faith had never been more nervous in her life. She wished Adrian were here. She could use his solid presence beside her to bolster her courage.

Caroline checked the contents of the refrigerator, made a few notes in her folder and asked, "How's it going?"

"As well as can be expected." Faith kept her hands still, trying not to fidget.

"Can you elaborate a little more?"

Faith wasn't sure what the woman wanted to know. "Kyle didn't have much of an appetite yesterday, but he ate a good breakfast this morning. He adores the alpacas, especially the baby. He misses his friends and his foster parents. We went to the phone booth yesterday evening and called his buddies, Tyrell and Dylan."

Should she mention Kyle woke in the night and was crying, or would that count against her?

"Did talking to the boys upset Kyle?"

"Maybe a little. It has to be hard being pulled from all he knew."

"Where is he now?"

"Upstairs in his room. Shall I get him?"

"We can go up together. I'd like to see his room now that he's settled."

Faith led the way up the narrow fight of stairs to the bedroom opposite hers. She opened the door to Kyle's room expecting to see him reading or coloring at his desk. He wasn't in the room. His bedroom window stood wide open with the screen pushed out.

She rushed to the window. The porch roof beyond was empty. The limbs of the old oak beside the house overhung the porch offering an adventurous boy a way down to the ground.

"He's gone." Faith heard the panic in her voice as she turned to the social worker.

Miss Watkins said, "Maybe he came downstairs and we didn't notice."

It took only a few minutes to search the house and see he wasn't in it. Where could he be? Faith opened the front door and stepped onto the porch with Miss Watkins right behind her. Faith scanned the yard. At least Kyle wasn't lying unconscious on the ground beneath the tree.

"He's likely out in the barn with Shadow." She tried calling his name but got no answer.

Crossing to the barn, Faith pulled open the door and called him again. Still no answer.

Inside, she found Myrtle and Shadow lying together undisturbed. Copper dozed in her stall. Kyle wasn't in here. Faith's worry took flight like the pigeons fluttering in the rafters. Where could he be?

Caroline asked, "Did he talk about running away?"

"He hasn't run away. I'm sure he's playing nearby."

Why would he run away? Was she such a terrible parent that he couldn't bear to live with her?

Faith opened the back door of the barn and went out into the alpaca's pen. They were milling about near the gate to the orchard and looking in that direction. The gate was closed. Faith knew she had left it open that morning so they could go out to graze.

She cupped her hand around her mouth and shouted for Kyle.

"He's with me!"

The booming voice from the orchard belonged to Adrian. Faith relaxed. Kyle was safe if he was with Adrian.

When the pair emerged from the trees, Faith crossed her arms and scowled at her nephew. "Did you climb out your bedroom window?"

"Yes."

"Why would you do such a thing? You could have fallen and been badly hurt."

He glanced from her to Miss Watkins. "I'm sorry. I won't do it again."

Miss Watkins dropped to his level. "Kyle, why did you sneak out of the house?"

He shrugged. "I don't know."

She laid a hand on his shoulder. "I understand that this is very difficult for you. If you aren't happy here, it's all right to tell me."

Faith held her breath. Would this woman take Kyle away from her so soon? They had barely gotten to know each other.

"It's okay. Sometimes it's boring, but it's okay." His voice wobbled.

Adrian said, "Idle hands are the devil's workshop. The boy needs work to occupy his mind. He can help me pick peaches if he is bored."

A quick frown crossed Caroline's face, but she didn't say anything to Adrian as she rose. Instead, she patted Kyle's head. "I'll be back in a week to check on you. All right? You have your aunt call me if you need anything. Will you be okay until then?"

"I guess." He shoved his hands in the waistband of his jeans.

As Miss Watkins headed for her car, Faith turned to Kyle. "You may help Adrian gather fruit until lunchtime. I'll call you when it's ready."

Kyle ventured a small request. "Can we have burgers and French fries?"

As a reward for climbing out your window and scaring me half to death?

Faith put aside her fright and forgave the boy for his behavior. "I think I can manage that, but it won't be like the fast food you get from town. Adrian, would you care to join us?"

Would he accept? She didn't want to appear too eager for his company, but she had missed him the past several days.

"I reckon I can. My hay is cut and drying in the fields. I have no need to rush home."

"*Goot.* Kyle, you must do as Adrian says."

"I will." The boy's smile returned.

Adrian said, "There are some wooden boxes inside the barn door. Bring them out to the tree where we were working."

"You got it." Kyle took off at a jog.

Faith said, "It's kind of you to let him help."

"You look tired. Is everything all right?"

"Kyle has nightmares. I haven't been sleeping well, either."

"He's had it tough, poor tyke."

"When we unpacked his things, I saw he had a picture of his mother and father. He wanted it on his bedside table. I let him keep it." She chewed the corner of her lip. Would he think she had done the wrong thing by going against their Amish teachings? Photographs were considered graven images and thus banned from Amish homes.

"The boy is not Amish. He does not know our ways. Give him time to learn about the things we believe."

She nodded, pleased that Adrian's advice mirrored her own feelings.

He leaned close. "But don't tell the bishop's wife. You already have one strike in her book."

Faith held back a giggle as Kyle came through the barn, his arms filled with a tall stack of boxes. "Are these the ones you need?"

Adrian said, "*Ja,* those are the ones. Your *aenti* and I will earn a pretty penny if we can fill and sell this many boxes of peaches."

Kyle looked between them. "You should charge more than a penny."

Adrian laughed. "Your nephew has a head for business, Faith. Should we follow his advice?"

Pretending to consider it, she finally said, "I agree. I say we ask for a nickel."

Adrian ran his fingers down his chin whiskers. "Let's think big. We should ask for a dime."

Kyle scrunched up his face. "Are you making fun of me?"

Faith ruffled his hair. "Perhaps a little."

Kyle rolled his eyes. "Whatever."

Adrian said, "Come along. Our work is waiting."

Faith watched them walk away together with mixed emotions. Kyle would need the influence of a man in his life, someone to teach him how to earn a living and work the land. Was she wrong to hope that Adrian could fulfill that role? It was a lot to ask of a neighbor. Those were things a father should teach a son.

Adrian would make a great father. He was kind and patient. She'd never heard him utter an angry word. While she never intended to marry again, if she did, someone like Adrian would be the kind of husband she'd look for. Someone exactly like Adrian.

The idea of being his wife made her blush. She quickly dismissed it as a fantasy that could never come true. Adrian wouldn't marry again any more than she would. The love he held in his heart for his first wife didn't leave room for another.

Wishing things could be different was foolish. Daydreams about Adrian were a sure path to heartache. She knew that.

So why couldn't she put her foolish yearning away?

Chapter Eleven

Several days later, Faith rose at five o'clock. She dressed, brushed and rolled her hair, fastened on her *kapp* and went down to start a fire in the kitchen stove. Stacking kindling and newspaper inside the firebox, she put a match to it. When she was sure the fire was going, she closed the firebox door.

While the stove heated, she straightened up in the living room. Adrian would be over soon to start work in the orchard. She didn't want him to see her home in a state of disarray.

Grabbing her broom, she began sweeping the floors. Soon she would have to have the offending pink and white linoleum replaced. The bishop had generously given her eight months to convert the old *Englisch* house into an Amish home. A home for her and Kyle, where the ghosts of the past could be put to rest and their new lives could flourish. It wouldn't be easy, but it would be worth all her hard work.

She finished her floors, washed up and began making breakfast. At half-past five o'clock, Faith called to Kyle from the bottom of the stairs. "Kyle, time to get up. Breakfast is ready."

She had to call one more time before he appeared in the kitchen, his hair tousled and his eyes puffy with sleep. "What time is it?"

"Almost six o'clock, sleepyhead. We have a lot of work waiting for us."

"We do?" He sat at the table and yawned.

She loaded both their plates with pancakes and scrambled eggs and carried them to the table. "Adrian will be here soon to start picking peaches. You don't want to keep him waiting, do you?"

"No. Is Miss Watkins coming today?" Kyle folded his arms on the table and laid his head down.

"Not that I know of."

"Good."

Outside, a loud whinny came from the barn. Faith said, "Sounds like Copper is wanting her breakfast, too."

Kyle raised his head to squint at Faith. "Can I feed her?"

"*Ja,* but first eat before your eggs get cold." Faith sat beside him, bowed her head to say a quick silent prayer and then began eating.

"Can I feed Shadow, too?" Kyle forked in a mouthful of eggs.

"His mother will give Shadow all he needs for a few months yet, but we need to feed her."

"Okay. Then can I play on the swing Adrian made me yesterday?"

Adrian had turned a length of rope and a broad plank into a swing that now hung from the oak tree beside the porch. Faith said, "After all your chores are done."

"What chores?"

"We must feed the horse and turn her out to graze. We must feed and water the chickens and gather their eggs."

"Then can I play?"

"Not until we feed the alpacas, clean up their pen, pick the debris out of their coats and let them out to graze."

"How long will that take?"

"It takes as long as it takes, Kyle."

It might sound like a lot of work to him now, but wait until next spring when there would be a garden to hoe and weeds to be pulled every day and all before he went to school. Faith smiled. Amish children did not have time to be bored.

Kyle finished his breakfast and waited impatiently for Faith to wash the dishes. When they were done, he dashed ahead of her to the barn. "Remember the rules," she called out.

He immediately slowed down. "Don't run behind a horse and always speak softly to let them know where you are."

"Very *goot*."

She passed Adrian's farm wagon sitting in the shade. The bed of the wagon was half full of boxes of peaches. The scent of the ripe fruit filled the still morning air. Today they would load the rest of the wagon and head into the farmer's market in Hope Springs where Faith hoped her fruit would fetch a good price.

She opened the barn door, and Kyle ducked under her arm to get inside ahead of her. He made a beeline for Shadow's stall. His little buddy rushed away to hide beneath his mother.

Faith showed Kyle how to measure and pour the feed into the troughs for the alpaca. While Myrtle was busy with her breakfast, Shadow ventured close to Kyle and allowed the boy to pet him.

Kyle's bright grin gladdened Faith's heart. She took a small rake and a shovel from their place on the wall and handed them to the boy.

He said, "What's this for?"

"To *redd-up* the stall. To clean it." She indicated the manure piles.

He wrinkled his nose. "Yuck!"

She folded her arms and scowled at him. "Shadow is your responsibility. You said you would take care of him. Do you want him to sleep on a messy floor?"

"No."

She held out the tools. He approached with lagging steps and took them from her. Faith had trouble holding back her laughter as he carefully raked the manure onto the flat shovel. He looked at her. "Now what?"

"I will fetch the wheelbarrow. When we have done everyone's stall we will empty it onto the pile behind the barn."

"We're keeping it? Why?"

"Because it will make very *goot* fertilizer for the orchards and gardens next spring."

It took most of an hour to feed all the animals and clean the stalls. To Faith's delight, Kyle didn't complain or shirk from the work. They let Myrtle and Shadow out into the pen. Shadow raced about in delight at finding himself outside.

Faith and Kyle were crossing back to the house when she saw Adrian striding toward them across the field. He was pulling a small wagon behind him.

He raised a hand and waved. Her heart flipped over with unexpected joy at the sight of him.

Kyle took off toward him. "Hi, Adrian. I cleaned out the barn and fed all the animals and Shadow let me pet him."

Adrian grinned at Kyle. "Then you have done a man's work already this morning. You must be tired."

"No. Well, maybe a little."

"You deserve a rest." Adrian picked the boy up and balanced him on his shoulder. Kyle's squeal of fear quickly turned into giggles of delight.

Faith waited until the two of them caught up with her before falling into step beside them. Adrian immediately shortened his stride to match hers. Something Mose had never done.

She needed to stop comparing the two men in her mind. There was no comparison.

"Aunt Faith says we are going to town later. Are we?"

"We are. It is Market Day. Almost everyone goes to town on Market Day."

"Cool beans. Can you teach me to drive the horse?"

By this time they had reached the porch. Adrian swung Kyle down and deposited him on the steps. "Someday, but not today. We must take my team and they are too big for you to handle."

"I'm strong." Kyle flexed one arm and pushed up his sleeve to show his muscles.

Adrian whistled his appreciation. "We must put those muscles to work in the peach orchard. Are you ready?"

Kyle fisted his hands on his hips. "*Ja*. I'm ready."

Faith pressed her hand to her lips to hide her smile. "Spoken like a true Amishman."

Adrian folded his arms over his chest. "Grab a couple of boxes from the big wagon and put them in this one. We won't have to carry our peaches so far this way. Can you pull this out to the tree where we stopped working yesterday?"

"Sure." The boy took off at a run, the little wagon bouncing behind him.

Faith spoke softly to Adrian. "He has taken quite a liking to you. God was wise to bring you into his life."

"He is a fine boy. He reminds me of my son."

Faith laid a hand on Adrian's arm. "This must be very difficult for you."

Adrian waited for the pain of his son's loss to strike his heart, but it didn't. Instead, he recalled the way Gideon had always wanted to help, sometimes to the point of being in the way. Kyle had the same burning desire to prove his worth.

Adrian glanced at Faith's small hand on his arm. Her touch was warm and comforting. Was she right? Did God have a purpose for bringing him into Kyle's life?

For the past several years Adrian had thought only of what

he had lost. He'd never once considered that God might use him as a gift to others.

He gazed into Faith's sympathetic eyes. "Kyle reminds me of Gideon, but he is not Gideon. I see in Kyle a boy with joys and pain, hopes and fears that are all his own. I'd like to think that they would have been friends. I know Lovina would have liked having you for a neighbor."

"I wish I could have known her."

"Me, too."

Adrian moved away from the comfort Faith offered. "We'd better get busy or we'll miss the start of the market."

"You're right. I need the best possible price for my fruit. My yarn is selling fairly well, but not well enough." They began walking toward the orchard.

"I've been thinking about that. Have you any items you'd like to sell at the market?"

"You mean things made from my yarn? I have several baby blankets and two dozen socks ready. Should I take them?"

"Many tourists come for the quilt auction that will be held this afternoon. They might buy your work."

She shook her head. "My plain socks hardly compare to the beautiful quilts they come to buy."

They reached the gate leading into the orchard. Kyle joined them carrying more boxes than he could safely manage. Shadow was prancing and bouncing beside him.

Adrian opened the gate for him. As usual, the curious alpacas came galloping up to investigate this new activity.

Kyle petted his little buddy. "I wish Shadow could come to town with us. I bet he'd like it."

Faith chuckled. "The tourists would stare at an alpaca riding in an Amish buggy, that's for sure."

Adrian stopped in his tracks. "They would, wouldn't they?"

Faith and Kyle walked on until they noticed he wasn't following. Faith stopped and looked back. "What's the matter?"

"Kyle and Shadow have given me an idea."

"We have?" Kyle looked perplexed.

"A very good idea. Faith, can you bring your spinning wheel to market and spin yarn while others are watching you?"

"*Ja*. What are you getting at?"

"Could we take Shadow to town with us?"

She shook her head. "He's only a few days old. It wouldn't be good for him to be separated from his mother for any length of time."

Adrian pondered the problems involved in his scheme. "And Myrtle is known for her spitting skills. That wouldn't work."

Faith's eyes lit up. "You want to take one of the alpacas to market with us as an advertisement for my yarns."

"You said it yourself. People would stop and stare. They might also stop and buy. Which of your animals has the best temperament?"

"Socks," she said without hesitation. "She loves attention and she loves people."

He nodded. Socks was the least likely to spit on an unsuspecting customer. "Would she follow behind the wagon into town?"

Faith's face showed her growing excitement. "I don't see why not. She's halter trained."

He held up his hand. "What's wrong with this plan?"

Faith shrugged. "Nothing that I can see."

Adrian nodded slowly. "Kyle and I will get started on the peaches. You get together the things you'd like to sell."

He turned and scratched Socks between the ears. "Looks

like you're going to town, girl. What do you think about that?"

Kyle ran ahead with the wagon into the orchard with Shadow hot on his heels.

Faith once again wore her best bonnet and Sunday dress as she sat on the high seat of Adrian's wagon. Kyle sat between them as excited as any six-year-old child on his way to a special treat. The boy had been awed into silence by the size of Adrian's draft horses but soon recovered his chatty nature.

As they approached Hope Springs, they met dozens of other Amish families all heading in the same direction. The influx of lumbering produce-laden wagons and buggies forced the traffic in town to drop to a crawl. The slow pace allowed many drivers and their passengers to gawk at Socks as she ambled along behind Adrian's wagon.

The alpaca didn't seem at all upset by the commotion going on around her. With her head held high, she surveyed the activity with wide, curious eyes.

Adrian turned off Main onto Lake Street. "The regular weekly markets are held every Friday afternoon in a large grassy area next to the lumber yard up ahead."

"Is it all produce?"

"You will find a wide range of fruits and vegetables sold here including certified organic produce. There will also be homemade baked goods, homemade jams, local honey, meat, eggs and cheeses. You can even find fresh cut flowers as well as fresh and dried herbs and spices."

Faith could already see the striped canopies of numerous tents being set up. "I'm surprised at the size, given the fact that Hope Springs isn't that big of a town."

"This isn't a regular market day. This is our Summer Festival. It's held every year on the last day of August. The big draw this year is the Quilts of Hope charity quilt auction. My mother mentioned that they have over fifty quilts to sell."

Adrian maneuvered his wagon to a tent marked for fresh produce and fruit. With Faith and Kyle's help, he began unloading the wagon and stacking their boxes of peaches in neat rows inside the tent. The work would have gone faster if not for the crowd of children and adults who quickly gathered around Socks. Faith answered numerous questions about her animal while helping Adrian and keeping an eye on Kyle.

When they had the wagon unloaded, Adrian parked the wagon near a row of buggies and unhitched his team. He slipped off their bridles and put halters on the pair but left them in their harnesses. He turned to Faith. "Where would you like to set up your spinning wheel?"

"I wish I had a tent." The afternoon sun beating down on her head promised to make her demonstration hot work unless she could find some shade.

"*Ja,* we need to get one for you."

Faith liked the way he said "we," as if they would be doing this together again.

Kyle pulled at her sleeve. "Can I go look around?"

On one hand, she was as eager to explore all the tents and displays as Kyle was, but on the other hand, she didn't want Adrian to be stuck looking after Socks. The alpaca was her responsibility.

She put aside her childish desires and said, "Perhaps Adrian can show you around."

Kyle turned his pleading eyes toward Adrian. "Can you? Please?"

"I must stay with the wagon," he replied.

Faith wasn't about to let him miss out on a fun afternoon. "Socks belongs to me. I will stay with her. Please take Kyle and show him the sights."

A young man made his way though the crowd and straight

to Socks. "So this is an alpaca! They are cute. Is this the one that spit on you and the bishop's wife?"

The resemblance between the two men was unmistakable. Faith wasn't surprised when Adrian said, "Faith, this is my *bruder,* Ben."

Ben's grin lit up his face. He touched the brim of his straw hat. "I'm pleased to meet you, Faith Martin."

She bowed slightly. "I'm pleased to meet you, as well. Myrtle was the ill-mannered one. This is Socks. She likes people."

"May I pet her?" Ben asked.

Faith nodded. Ben reached out hesitantly and stroked his hand along Socks's jaw. She showed her appreciation by stepping close and wrapping her long neck around him in a hug.

From behind her, Faith heard a pair of girls' voices cooing in unison. "Isn't that sweet?"

The girls, identical twins, joined Ben in petting Socks. Adrian spoke to his brother. "Ben, would you mind watching Socks while Faith and I show Kyle around?"

Ben winked at Adrian. "Not a bit."

"Danki." Adrian looked to Faith and tipped his head toward the nearest tent. "Shall we?"

She nodded and reached for Kyle's hand. As she grasped it, he let out a hiss of pain. Startled, she let go. "Did I hurt you?"

He put his hands behind his back and shook his head. Adrian squatted to his level and said sternly, "Let me see."

Reluctantly, Kyle extended his hands. There were large blisters on both palms.

Faith sucked in a sharp breath knowing how painful they had to be. "Kyle, why didn't you tell me you'd hurt yourself?"

"I was afraid you would make me stay home."

She thought of all the raking and wheelbarrow pushing

he'd done as well as the heavy boxes full of peaches he'd pulled through the orchard in the little wagon. Never once had he complained.

"Darling, you mustn't be afraid to tell me when something hurts. We need to find somewhere to wash these and put some bandages on them."

Ben said, "There's a first-aid tent near the front of the lumber yard."

Faith flashed him a grateful smile. "*Danki*. Come along, Kyle. We'll get you fixed up in no time."

She and Adrian guided him through the crowds to the tent run by the local firefighters. A kindly fireman rinsed Kyle's hands, applied an antiseptic cream and a large Band-Aid to each palm. When he was done, he gave Kyle a lollipop. "For being so brave."

Faith thanked him. He said, "No problem. If you go out behind this tent you'll see we are providing free pony rides to all the children attending the market today. Our police and fire departments are giving out snow cones and popcorn, too."

Kyle looked hopefully at Faith. "Can I ride a pony?"

He certainly deserved some fun after all the work he'd done. "You may."

They found the ride without difficulty. Kyle waited patiently until it was his turn. Adrian lifted him aboard a small white horse and stepped back beside Faith as he and several other Amish children went round and round on the plodding ponies.

Standing beside Adrian and watching Kyle enjoying himself, Faith had a glimpse of what her life might have been like if she had married the right man and been blessed with children of her own.

While she might never be a wife again, she now had a chance to raise a son. The thought was bittersweet.

After the ride came to an end, they walked on together exploring the various tents and booths until they came to the largest tent. Two sides of the tent had been rolled up to take advantage of the gusty breeze. Inside, dozens of beautifully crafted quilts hung from wooden frames meant to display them to full advantage. The room was already crowed with *Englisch* men and women examining the quilts closely.

Faith was admiring a wedding ring quilt pattern done in cream, pinks and blues when she spotted Nettie Sutter, Adrian's mother and several other women conferring at a table near the back of the tent.

"Adrian, there's your mother."

"Where?"

She pointed. He quickly turned the other way and took her arm. "Let's go. I don't need any quilts."

Chapter Twelve

Adrian hoped to avoid his mother's too-sharp eyes but he should have known better. She had already seen them and was headed in their direction with Rebecca Beachy holding on to her arm. His mother's cheeks were rosy red from exertion. Wisps of her gray hair had escaped from beneath her *kapp*.

"Adrian, you are just what we need—a strong son to help me set up these tables. Hello, Faith." His mother's eyes darted between the two of them with intense speculation. No doubt she had already jumped to the wrong conclusion about his business association with Faith.

He said, "We've brought peaches to sell."

She winked at him. "What a clever excuse to bring Faith to our market. Faith, I'd like you to meet Rebecca Beachy. She and her aunt are neighbors of mine. Although Rebecca is blind, she stitches beautiful quilts."

Rebecca held out her hand. "My talent comes from God, it is not of my own making."

Faith stepped forward and took Rebecca's hand. "I'm pleased to meet you."

Rebecca tipped her head to the side. "And who else do you have with you?"

Adrian saw Kyle peeking from behind Faith's skirt.

Faith urged the boy forward. "This is my *Englisch* nephew, Kyle."

Kyle frowned up at her. "I'm not English, I'm from Texas."

Adrian's mother chuckled. "It's nice to meet you, Kyle from Texas."

"Have you had a pony ride yet?" Rebecca asked.

He nodded. "Aunt Faith says I can have a snow cone, too."

Rebecca grinned. "*Ach,* I love them. You must try the pineapple ones. They're the best."

"Adrian, can you spare a few minutes to help us?" his mother asked.

He looked over the number of visitors filing through the tent. This would be the best place for Faith to set up her wheel. "If I may ask a favor in return?"

Mamm nodded. "Of course."

"May Faith use one of your tables to sell her yarn?"

His mother grinned at Faith. "I don't see why not. The more, the merrier. Show Adrian where you want to set up."

Within a few minutes he'd set up the tables his mother needed and placed one for Faith near the open side so that Socks could be tethered out on the grass. His mother promised to keep an eye on Kyle while he and Faith returned to the wagon to collect Faith's spinning wheel and the yarns she had boxed up to sell.

They found the wagon surrounded by a dozen young Amish girls admiring Socks. Ben, seated casually on the tailgate of the wagon, was clearly enjoying the attention.

Faith and Adrian shared an amused glance before Adrian stepped inside the circle of young women. "*Danki,* Ben, I'll take over now."

Standing up, Ben said, "I don't mind watching Faith's pet a little longer."

"If you want to be useful, little *bruder,* you can carry Faith's spinning wheel to the tent where the quilts are being auctioned."

"I can handle that if one of you girls can show me the way." Ben's charming smile gathered him several volunteers.

After Ben left, Adrian stacked together Faith's wares and carried the boxes while she led Socks through the maze of vendor stalls back to the quilt tent.

Adrian staked Socks's lead rope just outside the tent. The alpaca promptly lay down in the thick green grass.

Kyle was waiting for them with a snow cone in his hand. Adrian's mother sat beside him enjoying one, too.

Kyle held his out. "These are really good. You should get one, Aunt Faith."

Faith said, "I hope you thanked Mrs. Lapp."

"I did." He slurped at juice dripping over the paper holder.

Adrian's mother rose and came to stand beside Faith. "He's been well behaved. Is this one of your alpacas? They are cute."

She leaned closer, and Adrian heard her ask, "Is this the one that spit on the bishop's wife?"

Faith blushed a becoming shade of pink. "No."

He took pity on her and tried to distract his mother. "*Mamm,* do you need anything else?"

"Not that I can think of," she replied.

"Faith, can I do anything else for you?" he asked. He needed to get back to the produce and see that it sold for a decent price, but he didn't want to leave her side. He was happy when he was near her.

She smiled sweetly at him. "I will be fine, *danki.*"

He turned to Kyle. "You must keep an eye on Socks while your *aenti* is busy and don't wander off without telling her."

"Okay." Kyle took his snow cone and went out to sit in the

grass beside Socks. A number of people had already gathered to stare at the unusual creature. When they saw Kyle sit beside her, they pressed in for a closer look.

Faith, having arranged her yarns by color in small baskets on the table, sat down at the spinning wheel and began pumping the pedals that made it turn. Adrian stood back and watched to see how she would handle being on display along with her work. He didn't have long to wait.

A middle-aged *Englisch* woman with her husband stopped to watch Faith spin. She asked, "Is this all handmade yarn?"

"*Ja,* from my own alpacas." She seemed so nervous. Adrian wondered if he'd made a mistake in suggesting the venture.

The man asked, "What type of dye do you use?"

Faith glanced to Adrian. He gave her a thumbs-up sign.

She turned back to the prospective buyers. "Alpacas come naturally in twenty color variations. I have white, fawn, brown, gray and black, with many shades in between. The fleece dyes beautifully if you'd like colors other than these natural shades."

Nettie Sutter stepped up to the table. "I've heard it's better than wool."

"Alpaca has a softness unlike any other natural fiber. Most people find it doesn't itch like sheep's wool. It is also very lightweight and yet is warmer than wool. I have a receiving blanket made from white alpaca that you might be interested in for Katie's baby when it arrives." She indicated a box at the end of her table.

Adrian could see that the more Faith talked about her alpacas and her spinning, the more relaxed she became.

Nettie withdrew the blanket and gushed, "This is wonderfully soft. Feel it." She held the blanket out to the *Englisch* woman. She exclaimed over the quality, too. In a matter of minutes Faith made her first sale. Adrian turned to leave and found his mother at his side.

She said, "I like your new neighbor."

He scowled at her. "That's all Faith is. A neighbor. Nothing more."

A smug look settled over his mother's features. "Isn't that what I said?"

"What you say and what you mean are often two different things."

She patted his arm as if he were a child. "Now you sound like your father. Go and take care of your peaches. Don't worry. I will keep a close eye on your neighbor and her child. I think it's about time I got to know them better."

Chapter Thirteen

On Sunday morning Faith entered the home of Adam Troyer, the handyman in Hope Springs. His house had been chosen for the preaching service. Kyle was at her side.

She glanced down at him. It would be a long morning for a boy who wouldn't be able to understand the Pennsylvania Dutch preaching or the readings from the German Bible. How would he handle it? In the five days that he'd been with her he seemed to be adjusting well, but this might be stressful for him.

Sitting on a bench on the women's side of the aisle, she looked Kyle in the eyes. "You must sit on that side with the men today."

"But I want to stay with you."

"You are too old to sit with the women. I'll be right here. You must be quiet and respectful as we talked about last night. Amish children do not make a fuss, even when they are bored or tired."

"But I don't want to sit by myself," he whined.

"The boy can sit with me."

Faith glanced up to see Adrian standing beside them. She couldn't control the rush of happiness that swept though her. Even Kyle's face brightened.

He said, "Hi, Adrian. I didn't know you were going to be here."

Faith nodded her appreciation for Adrian's offer to sit with Kyle. "*Danki,* Adrian."

His gaze settled on her face. Heat filled her face, and she knew she was blushing. She looked away determined to control the intense longing that took over whenever he was near.

No matter how often she told herself a match between them was impossible, her desire to spend time with Adrian grew stronger, not weaker.

Adrian placed his hand on Kyle's shoulder. "Come along. We must find our place."

He led the boy away and found a seat near the back of the room in case he had to take the boy outside. He wasn't sure how Kyle would act during the long, solemn service.

Amish children were taught from infancy to keep quiet during Sunday preaching. Amish mothers usually brought a bag of ready-to-eat cereal or snacks to help occupy the *kinder* who became restless. Adrian wished he'd thought of bringing something for Kyle.

Throughout the service, Adrian remained acutely aware of Faith across the room from him. There was a look of serenity on her face as she listened to the Word of God.

Her sweet voice blended well with the congregation when the hymns began. She sang almost as well as his cousin Sarah. Both women had received the gift of song from the Lord.

Adrian was no songbird. His wife used to joke that he couldn't carry a tune in a wooden bucket if his life depended on it. He joined the congregation for each and every hymn, but he kept his voice soft and low enough not to trouble his neighbors' ears.

To Adrian's relief, Kyle remained well behaved. During the second hymn, he stood on the bench to better view the hymnbook Adrian held. The pages contained only the words of each hymn in German. The melody itself had been passed down from generation to generation in an unchanging oral tradition that reached back hundreds of years.

During the second hour of preaching, Adrian noticed Kyle's head nodding as he struggled to stay awake. He wasn't the only one. Several of the elderly members and a few of the youngsters were having trouble, too. Adrian slipped his arm around Kyle's shoulders and pulled him against his side. Kyle soon dozed off.

From across the aisle, Faith caught Adrian's eye. Her soft smile encompassed both he and the boy. It was the kind of smile that made a man feel special. Made him want to earn more of them.

At the end of the service, Bishop Zook rose and faced the congregation. He read off the names of the young people who wished to be baptized into the faith two weeks from today. Adrian recognized all the names. He knew them and their families. He had watched them grow up. All of them were making the commitment after having experienced something of the outside world during their *rumspringa*. Like himself, most of them were ready to marry and start families of their own.

None of them had any idea of the heartaches that might await them.

Bishop Zook said, "And now I have one more matter to place before you. Our sister, Faith Martin, has come among us seeking to practice the faith of her fathers with piety and humility. She has asked to become a member of our congregation. As you know, this decision is not up to me alone. Therefore, I ask this question of all. Is there anyone who knows a just reason why this sister should not become one of us?"

Silence filled the meeting room. Adrian glanced at Faith. Her eyes were downcast as she awaited the verdict. The bishop's wife shifted in her seat but didn't stand up. No one spoke.

After a few moments, the bishop smiled broadly and said, "Come forward, Sister Faith. In the name of the Lord and the Church, I extend to you the hand of fellowship. Be ye a faithful member of our church."

Adrian relaxed. No one had spoken against her. Faith stood and walked to stand before the bishop. He took her hand, but because she was a woman, he then gave her hand to his wife who greeted her with a Holy Kiss upon her cheek.

Faith was now a member of their community and subject to all the rules of their faith. Adrian glanced at the boy sleeping against his side. She would have to raise Kyle in the ways of the faithful. It was a good life, and he was happy for the boy.

When the services came to an end a few minutes later, Adrian woke Kyle, and the two of them followed the other men outside. Kyle yawned and squinted up at Adrian. "I'm hungry."

"We'll eat soon."

Faith approached them. Happiness radiated from her face. She said, "Kyle, you were very well behaved today."

"I fell asleep," he admitted.

Her happy smile made her even prettier this morning. Adrian said, "Congratulations."

"*Danki.* Kyle, why don't you come with me now and let Adrian visit with his friends."

Other members of the church crowded around to offer their congratulations and welcome. Adrian stepped aside. It was her special day, and he was glad for her.

Because it was such a beautiful day, the meal was set up outdoors. The younger people soon had a volleyball net set up between two trees on the lawn. A dozen of the boys and girls quickly began a game. The cheering and laughter from both participants and onlookers filled the late summer afternoon with joyous sounds. Faith sat on a blanket in the grass with Kyle beside her. They were cheering for the girls.

"She has the makings of a good mother, don't you think?"

Adrian looked over his shoulder to find his cousin Sarah observing him with interest. She'd always had an uncanny knack for knowing what he was thinking. He didn't pretend ignorance.

"She is good with the boy."

Sarah settled herself on the tailgate of the wagon beside him. "Faith tells me that you have been good for the boy, too."

"He reminds me of Gideon."

Sarah cocked her head to the side as she studied the boy. "A little maybe because of his red hair, but Kyle's hair is darker and curlier. Is she going to send him to our Amish school or to an *Englisch* one?"

"I don't know."

"You haven't asked her?"

"It's none of my business." He looked down to pretend he didn't care one way or the other.

"That's odd."

"What is?" he muttered.

"It's just that the two of you seem so close."

He slanted a glance her way. "What's that supposed to mean?"

"The two of you seem close, that's all. You've been working at her farm since the day she moved in. People notice."

"People should mind their own business."

"You know that's not going to happen. You're single. She's single. She's a member of our church district now. There's nothing wrong with courting her."

He drew back in shock. "Is that what you think I'm doing?"

"Me? No, of course not. I know you better than that."

Mollified, he said, "I should hope so."

"You're being kind, that's all."

"Exactly."

"What your mother or others think is beyond my control."

"Mother thinks I'm courting Faith? I will straighten her thinking out on the way home, today."

"Before you do that, let me ask you something. Has your mother invited any single women to your family dinners recently?"

He thought back over the past month and realized she hadn't. "No."

"See."

"See what?" He couldn't follow her reasoning.

"Kindness brings its own reward."

"Speak plain, Sarah. What are you hinting at?"

She patted his arm. "All I'm saying is that while you are being kind to your neighbor, your mother has stopped searching high and low for someone to catch your interest."

"That's not my reason for helping Faith."

"I'm not suggesting it is. You have a kind heart, and Faith needs all the help she can get until she has her yarn business up and running well."

"That's right."

"It would be okay if you did decide to court her."

He looked into Sarah's eyes. "I don't know if I can take that chance again."

She laid a hand on his arm. "You can, otherwise you will miss out on something special. Lovina wouldn't want you to waste your life grieving for her. You know that. She is happy with God in heaven. She wants you to be happy, too."

"What if something happens to Faith or to Kyle? How could I live through such a loss again?"

"Adrian, you can do one of two things. You can blame God

for your misery or you can turn to Him and draw strength from His love. He is always there for us."

"You make it sound so easy. It isn't."

"Answer me this. Were you better off before you met Faith?"

"Nee."

"If you were given one and only one chance to kiss her, would you take it?"

He would take it in a heartbeat. *"Ja."*

"Then why are you turning down the chance to love her for a lifetime?"

He had no answer for Sarah, but she didn't seem to expect one. With a pat on his arm, she left to join Faith and Kyle on their quilt.

As was his custom, Adrian left the gathering early, went home and cut flowers from his garden. On his way to the cemetery, he pondered his feelings for Faith, what they meant and what he was willing to do about them. Did he have a chance to love her for a lifetime? Was that really within his grasp? The thought excited and frightened him. What if he loved and lost her, too?

At his wife's graveside, he laid the new flowers over the dried husks of the old ones. He stared at her headstone, but he was at a loss for something to say.

Turning away, he took his usual seat and leaned forward with his elbows braced on his thighs. Suddenly, the words came pouring out. "I never meant it to happen, Lovey. I wasn't looking for someone to care about. In my whole life I never wanted to share my hopes and dreams with anyone but you."

Until now. Until Faith. He raised his face to the sky. "Is this wrong? How can it be wrong to care about such a good woman? Faith is a good woman, a strong woman, but she needs someone to take care of her and her boy."

And I need someone to care about me.

Wasn't that the truth he'd been hiding from?

Adrian closed his eyes. "I've been dead inside for a long time. Waking up is painful, Lovey. I'm not sure I can do it."

Chapter Fourteen

Faith sat at her kitchen table with her checkbook in front of her on Thursday morning. She'd been able to pay her outstanding bills with the money she'd made at the market and she still had money left over. Her small bank account was growing at last.

In her wildest dreams she hadn't imagined doing this well so quickly. She'd sold all the yarn she'd taken with her to the market and had taken orders for several dozen additional skeins plus eight of her white baby blankets. She would have to redouble her spinning and knitting efforts to keep up.

Adrian's mother had invited Faith to join their co-op group and display her handmade wares each week on market day. With the cool days of fall not far away, yarn for warm socks, sweaters and mittens were sure to be in high demand.

Kyle came running into the room. He stopped beside Faith to grab a leftover breakfast biscuit from a plate in the center of the table. "My room is clean."

"*Danki,* Kyle."

"Is Adrian coming over today?"

She missed Adrian's presence as much as Kyle did. Maybe more. She'd gotten used to having him around. Some foolish part of her heart continued to hope that he'd come over with a new excuse to spend time with them, but it hadn't happened.

"I doubt it, dear. His work in the orchard is done. You will see him at the next preaching service."

"But that's another whole week away." Pieces of biscuit sprayed from his lips.

"Don't talk with your mouth full."

He swallowed. "I don't want to wait until church. Can't we go visit Adrian today?"

"No. Miss Watkins is coming today."

Faith hoped his sudden pout wasn't going to lead to a temper tantrum. "Why is *she* coming?" he demanded.

"It's her job to find out if you are happy here. Are you happy?"

Confusion clouded his eyes. "Can I go play with Shadow?"

A pang of disappointment stabbed her. Why couldn't he answer a simple question? "You may, but try not to get dirty."

He darted outside, letting the screen door bang shut behind him.

Was he unhappy living with her? He seemed to be adjusting well to this new way of life. She had been worried those first few nights, but he'd not had a nightmare for the past week.

Faith closed her eyes and took a deep breath. Her new life in Hope Springs was turning into a dream come true. Kyle was with her. The church community had welcomed her with open arms. Her business was off to a great start, and her share of the peach money had been an added bonus.

"Through you, Lord, all things are possible. I humbly give thanks for Your blessings."

Little more than a month ago she had arrived in Hope Springs with barely enough to support herself. Now, she had enough to support Kyle, too. An important step toward his permanent adoption. Would his social worker think it was enough? The Amish were frugal people. Faith didn't need a large sum of money to live comfortably. Could Caroline Watkins be made to understand that?

An hour later, the sound of a car pulling into the yard alerted Faith to Miss Watkins's arrival. Faith opened the door and waited as Caroline came up the steps. "Good morning, Miss Watkins. Do come in. How are you?"

Caroline said, "I'm fine. This shouldn't take long today. I'll make a quick tour of the house and then I'd like to talk to you and Kyle separately. Is that all right?"

"Certainly." Faith took a seat at the kitchen table and waited. She tried to ignore the nervous dread that started gnawing at the inside of her stomach. She knew there was nothing to fear, but she was afraid anyway. This woman had the power to remove Kyle from her home.

Ten agonizing minutes later, Caroline came back into the kitchen with smile on her lips. "Everything seems in order, Mrs. Martin. How are you getting along with Kyle?"

Faith let out the breath she'd been holding. "It's going well. He works hard and plays hard. We went to the Summer Festival in Hope Springs last week, and I think he really enjoyed himself."

"That's great to hear. Where is Kyle?"

"He's down in the barn playing with Shadow, the baby alpaca. The two of them have become fast friends. Shadow is living up to his name for he follows Kyle around whenever the boy is near. Would you like me to go get him?"

"I'd rather talk to him alone." Caroline went out the door.

Faith began her preparations for making bread. Keeping busy was better than pacing the floor and wondering what was going on between Kyle and Miss Watkins. What if Kyle told her he didn't like it here? What if he complained that he had too much work to do? A dozen unhappy scenarios ran through Faith's mind. Her stomach rolled into a tight knot.

A few minutes later, Miss Watkins returned to the house. Faith dusted the flour off her hands, set her bread dough aside and turned around. "Are you finished already?"

Her worry knot doubled in size when she saw the green speckles on Miss Watkins's clothes. Myrtle had been at it again.

"I'm so sorry. I should have warned you about Myrtle." Faith wet a kitchen towel and handed it to Caroline.

Caroline wiped her face and brushed at her blouse. "Their spitting is a disgusting habit. I couldn't find Kyle. Where else might he be?"

"He said he was going to the barn."

"He isn't in the barn. I called but he didn't answer. He wasn't with the baby alpaca." She scrubbed at her shoulder.

"Perhaps he's in the orchard."

"Does he disappear like this often?"

"No, of course not." Faith rushed outside and began frantically calling for Kyle. She and the social worker made their way from one side of the orchard to the other without any sign of the boy.

When they arrived back at the house and saw Kyle hadn't returned, Faith said, "We should go to the neighbor's farm and see if he is there."

"Has he done that before?"

"No."

Miss Watkins pulled her cell phone from the pocket of her slacks. "Can you call them and see if he's there?"

"My neighbors are Amish. They have no phones."

Miss Watkins bit her lip, then opened her phone. "We are wasting valuable time. I'm going to notify the sheriff that we have a missing child."

* * *

Adrian lay on his back beneath his grain binder and loosened the last bolt holding the sickle blades in place. It came loose easily, and he lowered the bar to the ground. His cornfields would be ready to cut soon, and he needed to make sure his equipment was in good working order. Sharpening the sickle blades was his first priority.

"What ya doing?"

Adrian twisted his head around to see Kyle squatting beneath the equipment with him. "I'm getting my machinery ready to harvest corn. What are you doing?"

"I came to help you."

"You have, have you? Where is your *aenti* Faith?" Adrian wormed his way out from beneath his equipment with the long row of blades in hand. He looked eagerly toward the house, but he didn't see Faith anywhere.

He had stayed away from her the past few days because he knew if they came face-to-face, he wouldn't be able to hide his longing or his fears. He hadn't been ready for that. Was he ready now?

Kyle said, "She's at home with that mean social worker."

Faith wasn't here. Adrian tried not to let his disappointment show. He focused on Kyle. "You must not speak badly of others, Kyle. You must forgive them for the wrongs they do."

"Why?"

"Because that is what God commands us to do. Why do you say your social worker is mean?"

"'Cause social workers take kids away from their moms." Kyle glanced over his shoulder as if expecting to see one swooping down on him like a hawk.

"Where did you hear this?"

"Dylan and Tyrell told me."

The names weren't familiar. Adrian asked, "Who are they?"

"My friends in Texas. They were in foster care with me because a social worker took them away from their mom. They told me not to like Becky too much cause a social worker would come and take me away to a new place, and one did. Dylan and Tyrell had been in three foster homes so they knew it would happen and it did."

"Becky was your foster mother?"

Kyle nodded. "I liked her a lot.

Adrian sat on the steel tongue of his grain binder. "I'm sorry you were taken from someone you cared about, but I know that Faith loves you and she wants you to stay with her for a long time."

Kyle turned away from Adrian and patted the side of the machine. "What does this thing do?"

"This is a grain binder. It cuts cane or corn into bundles of livestock feed."

"How?

Adrian understood Kyle's reluctance to talk about matters that troubled him. Wasn't he the same way? Didn't he avoid talking about his family because it brought the pain back sharp as ever?

He said, "The machine is powered by this gasoline engine. My team pulls it through the field while I stand up here to guide them." He indicated a small platform at the front.

"Up here?" Kyle climbed the three metal ladder rungs and stood behind the slim railing that allowed the driver to lean against it and kept him from falling while he drove his team.

The boy grinned when he realized he was now taller than Adrian. He stretched his hands out pretending to hold the reins of a frisky team. "What do I do next?"

Adrian walked around to the side of the machine. "You

guide your team along the corn rows. This sickle bar cuts the thick stalks about a foot off the ground. The reel lays them evenly onto this wide canvas belt. The belt feeds the stalks into a mechanism that gathers them together into a bundle, then wraps it with twine and knots it."

"Then what?"

"You must decide. See that lever in front of you?"

"Yup." Kyle reached beneath the safety rail to grasp a metal handle.

"Pull it back and the bundle is kicked out the side of the machine where it will lay in the field until I come back and stack them into tepee-style shocks."

"Why make a tepee out of them?"

These were things Adrian would have explained to his son if Gideon has lived. It was part of being a father, teaching the children how to farm and wrest a living from the land.

Kyle wouldn't have anyone to teach him unless Faith chose to remarry.

Would she remarry for the boy's sake? The thought didn't sit well with Adrian. What if the man she chose was unkind to her or to Kyle the way her first husband had been? He knew a few Amish husbands who believed they should rule their families with an iron fist.

"Why build tepees with them?" Kyle asked again.

"Because they shed water if you put the bundles together in an upright position. As they dry and shrink, it allows more air to flow around the inside of the bundles and they dry better. I put about twenty bundles into each shock."

"What if I push this lever forward?"

"Then the machine dumps the bundles onto a trailer that is pulled behind me, and my brother stacks them together so we can haul them to the barn."

"I wish I had a brother. That would be cool."

"It is sometimes, but sometimes they can be a pain in the neck."

Kyle climbed down from his post. "Can I see Meg and Mick?"

The boy had taken a liking to Adrian's team and had begged to ride one on the way home from market. Adrian hadn't allowed it then as they were on the highway, but he saw no harm in it now.

"*Ja,* they are in the barn."

"Can I ride one of them? They are like ten times bigger than the ponies at the fair."

Adrian thought of all the work he had to finish. Put side by side with Kyle's eager face, Adrian found only one conclusion. The work could wait.

In the barn, Adrian opened the door to Meg's stall and led her out to the small paddock. He hoisted Kyle to her broad back. She was so wide that the boy's feet stuck out straight instead of being able to grip her sides.

Adrian said, "Wrap your hand in her mane."

"Won't that hurt her?"

"*Nee,* it will not, but it might keep you from falling off."

Grasping the halter, Adrian led the mare around the paddock. She walked slowly and carefully, as if aware of the precious cargo she carried.

Kyle grinned from ear to ear. "I can see all the way to Texas from up here."

"How's the weather down that way?"

Shading his eyes with one hand, Kyle said, "Sunny and hot."

After the third time around the corral, Adrian stopped Meg and held his hands up to Kyle. "Come along. I have much work to do. I must sharpen my sickle and get my binder back together and Meg wants to have a good roll in the dust."

"Okay." Kyle reluctantly left his high perch. They walked

back into the barn, leaving Meg in the pen where she promptly lay down, rolled onto her back and frolicked in the dust she raised.

As they passed her stall, Kyle looked at Adrian. "Do you want me to *redd-up* her stall?"

Tickled by Kyle's use of an Amish term, Adrian knew the boy would soon fit into their Amish ways and leave his *Englisch* past behind. He stared into Kyle's eyes and saw he was dying to please.

Adrian stroked his beard. "Reckon I could use a good stable hand now and again."

Puffing out his chest, Kyle asked, "Where's your wheelbarrow and your shovel?"

"I will get them for you."

When he returned with the requested tools and gave them to Kyle, Adrian leaned on the stall gate to watch the boy work. It took him a while, but he managed to rake up the mess and push the wheelbarrow back to Adrian.

Sighing heavily, Kyle said, "Alpacas are much easier to clean up after."

"They are not as big as Meg."

"No wonder Aunt Faith raises them instead of horses."

Adrian chuckled. "No wonder."

Kyle pulled at the Band-Aid on his palm. "It came loose."

Adrian bent down to see. He removed the bandages and looked at the angry red sores. "You should have told me they were hurting you."

"They don't hurt." Kyle put his hands behind his back.

"Lying is a sin, Kyle. I know you want to please and prove that you are a good helper, but Faith will have my hide if these get infected. Come up to the house and let's get them clean."

In the kitchen, Adrian gently washed Kyle's hands and

patted them dry. He applied an antiseptic cream to them and wrapped a length of gauze around each palm. "Is that better?"

Kyle flexed his fingers. *"Ja."*

"I think I may have a pair of gloves you can wear over them." He rose and led the way to Gideon's room. Opening the door, he experienced the same catch in his chest that always hit him when he stepped over this threshold. The room looked the same as the day his son had left it.

On the blue-and-green quilt that covered the bed lay a baseball glove and a carved wooden horse. Gifts meant for a birthday that had never arrived. Crossing the room, Adrian pulled open a dresser drawer and retrieved a small pair of knit gloves.

"Try these on." He turned to hand them to Kyle and froze. Kyle was on his knees by the bed galloping the toy horse across the quilt.

He grinned up at Adrian. "This looks like Meg."

Adrian held back the shout that formed in his throat.

Leave that alone. It belongs to my son.

He knew Kyle wouldn't understand. The boy meant no harm. He was simply doing what boys did—playing with a toy as it was meant to be played with.

Is this part of Your plan, Lord? Am I to see that I'm being greedy and selfish by hanging on to these things? Gideon would share his toys with this boy, I know he would. He had a kind heart like his mother.

Adrian forced a smile to his stiff lips. "I made it to look like Meg. I was going to make another one that looked like Mick."

"You made it? Cool beans." Kyle stared at the toy in awe.

"Would you like to have it?"

"Can I?" His eyes grew round.

"It is yours if you want it."

Kyle grinned. "Thanks. I mean, *danki.*"

"You're welcome. Now try these on." Adrian held out the gloves. They proved to be too small.

Knowing a pair of his would be much too large, Adrian said, "Try not to get dirty."

"That's what Aunt Faith tells me."

"Does it work?"

"Not so much."

Adrian smiled as he ruffled Kyle's hair and went outside to finish his work. He sharpened his blades while Kyle galloped little Meg across the workbench and jumped her over hammers and assorted tools. It felt good to have a child with him again.

He still missed his son, still wished it was Gideon with him, but he was able to enjoy Kyle's company and appreciate the boy for who he was.

Adrian was reattaching his sickle blades when the sound of a car coming up his lane drew his attention. He rose to his feet and saw the sheriff's white SUV roll to a stop in front of his house.

Adrian looked at Kyle seated on the ground beside him. "Does your aunt know you are here?"

The boy shrugged.

Adrian shook his head at his own thoughtlessness. "That is a question I should have asked an hour ago."

He held his hand out to Kyle. "Come. You have some explaining to do."

Reluctantly, Kyle rose and walked with Adrian toward the sheriff's vehicle. The passenger's door opened, and Faith rushed toward them, a look of intense relief on her face. In her hurry she stumbled and would have fallen if Adrian hadn't lunged forward to catch her.

He held her tight against his chest and breathed in the fresh scent of her hair. She fit perfectly against him. It felt so right to hold her this way. She looked up at him with wide, startled eyes. Eyes filled not with fear, but with the same breathless excitement she had awakened in him.

In that instant he knew she felt as he did. The next move was up to him. Did he dare risk his heart again?

Chapter Fifteen

Faith rested in the safety of Adrian's embrace, relishing the strength and gentleness with which he held her. Gazing up into his face, she saw his eyes darken.

Did he feel it too, this current between them that defied her logical, sensible mind?

How had it happened? How had she fallen in love with him?

He said softly, "Kyle is okay."

"I knew he would be if he was with you," she whispered. She and Kyle would always be safe if Adrian was with them. If only it could be this way forever. It couldn't. She knew that.

Adrian was still in love with his wife. She couldn't compete with a ghost.

Besides, she had to concentrate on Kyle. Finalizing his adoption had to be her top priority. Adding Adrian to the picture would only complicate and delay things.

Reluctantly, she left the comfort of Adrian's embrace and sank awkwardly to the ground beside Kyle. She gathered him close in a tight hug. "I was so worried when I couldn't find you."

He wrapped his arms around her neck and hugged her

back. Suddenly, he let go and stepped away. Faith saw he was looking at the sheriff and Miss Watkins as they approached.

Faith cupped his chin and turned his face toward her. "It's all right. You aren't in trouble."

The sheriff pushed his hat back with one finger. "Looks like the lost sheep has been found."

Miss Watkins clasped her hands together. "I am so sorry that we wasted your time, Sheriff Bradley."

"Don't be. I like a happy ending. I just wish all my calls were so easy."

Miss Watkins focused her attention on Kyle. "You frightened us very badly, Kyle. Why did you run away from home?"

"I didn't."

Faith accepted Adrian's hand as he helped her to her feet. She said, "Kyle, you must let me know when you are going to visit a friend or a neighbor."

"Okay."

Miss Watkins stepped forward with a sharp frown on her face. "What's wrong with your hands, Kyle?"

"I got some blisters. Adrian fixed me up. He gave me this horse." He held up the toy.

Glancing between the adults, Miss Watkins leaned down to Kyle's level. "How did you get blisters? Did you touch something hot?"

"No." He shrank away from her and toward Faith.

Faith said, "He got them cleaning out a stall and helping us with the peach crop."

Adrian spoke up. "He rubbed his bandages off cleaning one of my stalls. I washed his sores and redressed them. He'll be okay in a few days."

Holding out her hand, Miss Watkins asked, "May I see your blisters?"

Kyle buried his face in Faith's skirt and put his hands behind his back.

Turning his face up to hers, Faith smiled encouragingly at him. "Is it okay if I unwrap them?"

He held out his hands. Faith unwound the dressing from his right hand. Miss Watkins took a closer look, then said, "Okay. Kyle, why don't you go to the car with Sheriff Bradley. I bet he'll show you how the radio works."

The sheriff nodded toward his SUV. "Come on, Kyle. Would you like to turn on the flashing lights?"

Kyle glanced from Faith to Adrian. "Is it *verboten*?"

Faith exchanged an amused look with Adrian, then said, "It's not forbidden. It is okay for Amish boys to do such a thing."

Kyle followed the sheriff, but the worried expression lingered on his face.

Miss Watkins folded her arms. "I will be the first to admit that I'm not familiar with Amish ways, but to work a child of six until both his hands are covered in blisters is not acceptable."

Faith cringed before the social worker's anger. Fear stole her voice. Beside her, Adrian said, "The boy worked hard to prove that he belongs among us. We did not make him do this."

Caroline shook her head. "Be that as it may, I'm not convinced this is the best arrangement for Kyle."

"Please, don't take him away from me." Faith wanted to race to the car, grab her child and hold on to him so tightly that no one could take him from her. Adrian's hand settled on her shoulder holding her in place.

Caroline sighed heavily. "I don't want to take him away, Mrs. Martin, but I have to know that he's in a safe environment. I would be neglecting my job and Kyle's welfare if I placed him in a questionable home."

"I'll do anything you ask. Please, don't take him away," Faith pleaded.

"Ultimately that decision is up to a judge. I'm here to help make the adoption possible. I want you to rethink how much work a child of six should be doing. I'll be back to visit again next Friday. Before then, you will need to make a list of Kyle's chores. We can go over them together and see if we can agree on what's appropriate for his age."

"I can do that," Faith quickly assured her.

"Keep in mind that he's going to be in school. There will be even less time for him to do chores." She walked back to the sheriff's vehicle leaving Faith and Adrian alone.

Faith started to follow her, but Adrian caught her arm. "Faith, we need to talk."

"I can't. Not now."

His shoulders slumped in defeat. "All right. Go home and take care of your child."

She squeezed his hand. "Thank you, Adrian."

"For what?"

"For understanding." Faith left him and took a seat inside the sheriff's vehicle.

"Are you ready for your first day of school?"

Bright and early Monday morning Faith climbed into the buggy beside Kyle.

He hooked his thumbs through his new suspenders giving them a sour look. "Do I have to wear these? I look like a dork."

"You must dress plain now. All the boys will be wearing them."

"Are you sure?" He let them snap back against his chest.

"*Ja,* I'm sure. Do you like your hat?"

He raised his flat-topped straw hat with both hands and looked up at it. "It's okay. It's like the one Adrian wears."

"He wears suspenders, too."

"Yeah, he does, doesn't he?" That mollified him.

"Are you excited about school?"

He sat back and folded his arms over his chest. "No. Everyone's gonna think I'm stupid cause I can't speak Pennsylvania Dutch."

She folded her hands in her lap. "Kyle, you are learning our language just as the Amish children at school will be learning English. If you help them, they will help you and nobody will be stupid."

"Maybe." He didn't sound convinced.

Faith cupped his chin and raised his face so she could see his eyes. "I know this is hard for you, but school is not all bad. You will learn many good things. Do you like to play baseball?"

"Yes."

"Amish children also like baseball. When I was in school, we played it almost every day. Not in winter, of course. In the winter, we went sledding during recess."

"Really?" He looked at her with interest.

"Really."

"That sounds kinda cool."

She grinned. "It wasn't cool. It was downright cold." She poked his side making him giggle.

"Can I drive the buggy?" he asked.

"You may, but just to the end of the lane." Faith had no fear that Copper would bolt. The mare was well trained and placid. In fact, it was hard to get her into high gear anymore.

"Hold the reins like this." Faith demonstrated. Kyle was quick to copy her and soon had Copper moving down the lane. Faith sat ready to take the lines at the first sign of trouble. Thankfully, they reached the highway without incident.

"How'd I do?" he asked as he handed the reins back.

"Very well. You're a natural." She headed Copper down

the road toward the schoolhouse a mile and a half away. After today Kyle would be walking, but she wanted to make sure he could find his way. Besides, the first day of school was special for any child, and she wanted to be a part of it.

When the building came into view, she said, "We're almost there."

Kyle slumped in his seat again. "Do I have to go? I feel sick."

She understood the anxiety he was feeling, but she knew he would soon make new friends. Faith had met earlier with his teacher, Leah Belier. A young Amish woman in her early twenties, Leah seemed devoted to students and to helping them learn. She had promised she would do her best to help Kyle adjust to his new surroundings.

Faith stopped the buggy on the sloping lawn of the one-room schoolhouse. Several other buggies were tied up alongside the building. Children were already at play on the swing set and the long wooden teeter-totter.

Faith sensed Kyle's interest, but he moved closer to her. Before she could convince him to get down, Leah came out of the schoolhouse door and waved to Faith.

Faith returned her greeting. Kyle buried his face in Faith's lap. "Can we go home, please?"

Leah was quick to assess the situation and approached the buggy. "You must be Kyle King. I'm so glad to meet you. I was hoping you could help me this morning."

Kyle eyed her with suspicion. "How?"

"I need a strong young boy to ring the bell for me."

Looking past her, Kyle assessed the situation. "I guess I could do that."

"Wonderful. Faith, would you like to sit in on class today?"

"I would."

After securing Copper to the hitching rail, Faith walked

with Kyle to the school building where Leah waited for them. The teacher pointed to the bell rope hanging inside the door-way. "Give it a yank, Kyle. It's time to start our classes."

Gritting his teeth, Kyle pulled with all his might. The bell clanged loudly.

Leah clapped her hands. "Very good, Kyle. You're every bit as strong as you look. Now, I need someone to put pencils and papers on all the desks. Can you help with that?"

"Sure."

"*Danki*. That means thank you."

"I know."

"The papers and pencils are on the table behind my chair. The desk directly in front of mine belongs to you."

The other children began entering by twos and threes. Leah welcomed them all by their first names, asking after family members and previous students. It was clear she enjoyed her job.

Faith took a seat at the back of the room where several young mothers sat visiting with each other.

She stayed for the first hour of class, just long enough to make sure Kyle was going to be okay. Leah kept all the students well in hand as she switched back and forth between English and Pennsylvania Dutch to make sure everyone understood her instructions.

After leaving the school, Faith drove home and set to work spinning another batch of yarns. Once they were done, she would take them into town after she picked up Kyle. She had a special treat in store for him.

By early afternoon, she had several dozen skeins ready to be dropped off at Needles and Pins. She hitched up Copper again and arrived at the schoolhouse just as the main door opened and a rush of children poured out.

Kyle, grinning from ear to ear, skidded to a halt beside her and held up a piece of paper. "I drew a picture of Shadow. Did you know we're the only people in Hope Springs who have alpacas?"

She grinned at his enthusiasm. "I suspected as much."

"Anna Imhoff and her brothers want to come over and see Shadow. Can they?"

"Perhaps tomorrow. Today, we must go into town and celebrate."

"Celebrate what?"

"Your first day at school. It's a big deal and it calls for a celebration."

"What kind of celebration?"

"I'm treating you to supper at the Shoofly Pie Café."

"Can we get pizza?"

"That sounds perfect."

"*Goot.* That means good in Pennsylvania Dutch. I learned it and some more words, too."

"I'm pleased to hear your day wasn't wasted. Did you make some new friends?"

"Anna Imhoff wants to be my friend, but she's a girl."

"Girls can be friends, too."

"Her brother, Noah, started teasing me 'cause I can't talk Amish. Anna got mad and scolded him."

"Then she sounds like a very good friend to have. Did everyone play baseball at recess?"

His mood went from happy to dejected. "Yeah, but no one picked me for their team."

"You are little yet. I'm sure you'll play many games when you're older."

"Maybe if I got a glove."

Leah approached the buggy. "He did well, Faith. He needs to work on his sums and his reading, but overall he's a bright, friendly boy."

"Wonderful." It was a relief to know that Kyle was fitting

in. She had worried that the language barrier would make school unhappy for him.

Leah left to speak to other parents, and Faith turned Copper toward town. Once they reached Hope Springs, Faith dropped off her yarns at the fabric store and drove on to the Shoofly Pie Café.

She and Kyle entered the homey café and were instantly surrounded with the smell of baking bread, cinnamon and frying chicken. A young Amish girl came forward. "*Velkumm* to the Shoofly Pie café. My name is Melody. Would you like a table or a booth?"

"A booth," Kyle answered before Faith could say anything.

The waitress led them to one of the high-backed seats that lined the walls of the room. Faith slid into the nearest bench. Kyle scooted in opposite her and propped his elbows on the red Formica tabletop.

Suddenly, Kyle's eyes lit up. "It's Adrian."

The boy waved. Faith turned to see her neighbor entering the door. He raised a hand and waved back. He was carrying a small package wrapped in plain brown paper and tied with string.

He stopped beside their booth. Faith wished her heart would stop trying to gallop out of her chest each time he was near.

Kyle spoke up eagerly. "I went to school today."

Adrian grinned at him. "So I heard. How was it?"

"Pretty fun. I learned to count to ten in Amish and how to say please and thank you."

"Those are all good things to know." Adrian focused his gaze on Faith. "How have you been?"

Missing you madly. "Fine, and you?"

"Busy. I'll start cutting corn tomorrow if this nice weather holds."

She couldn't care less about the mundane details of his life. Just seeing his face brightened her day.

He asked, "May I join you?"

Surprised and delighted, she said, "Certainly."

Kyle scooted over to let him sit down. Adrian said, "I brought you a present, Kyle." He slid the package toward the boy.

"Why? It's not my birthday." Kyle tore open the wrapping to reveal a baseball mitt. It was too big for his hand, but he didn't seem to mind. "Cool. I've been wanting one like this forever."

Adrian smiled at him. "Happy first day of school."

Faith couldn't put her finger on it, but there was something different about Adrian today. He was more lighthearted, happier than she had seen him. She liked the change. She liked it a lot.

He met her gaze. "Every boy needs a good baseball glove."

She said, "You didn't need to spend money on Kyle. I could have gotten him one."

"It's an old glove I had lying around. I thought Kyle might put it to good use."

"I sure will. Now they won't pick me last." Kyle smacked his fist in the pocket.

Faith's heart warmed to see Kyle so excited and happy. She started to convey her thanks, but Adrian stopped her with a shake of his head. "It's nothing."

The look in his eyes said differently. Then it hit her. She reached across the table to lay her hand on Adrian's arm. "It was Gideon's glove, wasn't it?"

"It was, but now it is Kyle's." His glance settled on her nephew. It was easy to read the deep affection he had for the boy.

It was only when Adrian looked into her eyes that she

became unsure of his feelings. He said, "I know Kyle's adoption is your main priority right now, but when that's over, I'd like to talk about the future."

Faith pulled her hand away. The future? What was he suggesting? Did he have more plans for the farm, or was he suggesting they could have a future together? Her heart raced as her breathing quickened. "The hearing is the last day of this month."

He winced. "That is a long time to wait."

"Then perhaps you should come over this evening if it's important." She bit the inside of her lip as she waited for his reply.

"It is important to me and I hope to you. *Ja,* I will come by later."

"I'm having pizza," Kyle announced.

Adrian tweaked the boy's nose. "Sounds good to me. I like pepperoni and extra cheese."

"Me, too." Kyle looked at Faith. "What kind do you like, Aunt Faith?"

"I'll have whatever the two of you are having."

Food was the furthest thing from her mind at the moment. What was on Adrian's mind that couldn't wait? Did she dare hope he returned her feelings of affection, or was she tricking herself into imagining what wasn't there?

"You're late getting back from town," Ben said, as he finished greasing the wheels of the grain binder and wiped his blackened fingers on a piece of cloth lying on top of the machine.

"I had supper at the café. Are you done already?" Adrian checked his brother's work and found it satisfactory.

"*Ja.* When will you start cutting?"

"I took a walk through the corn this morning. I think it will be ready by the end of the week, if it doesn't rain."

"*Dat* wants to start on our fields early tomorrow. We should be done in four or five days. When we're finished, I can come and give you a hand."

"I always appreciate your help with the farm work." Could he trust Ben with an even more important task?

Adrian hooked his thumbs in his suspenders. He wasn't ready to reveal his intentions toward Faith to his family just yet. He wanted to know her feelings first. She had been adamant that she would not remarry. If those were her true feelings, he would respect them and never bring up the subject again.

He needed to speak to her alone, but he couldn't do that with Kyle listening in. Knowing the boy's penchant for turning up in the wrong place at the wrong time, Adrian didn't want to risk it.

The smart thing to do would have been to wait until the adoption was over or at least until the boy was in school tomorrow, but Adrian didn't want to wait another day to know if Faith cared for him as he'd grown to care for her.

Oh, he'd had every intention of waiting until the time was right…then she'd smiled at him in the café and laid her hand on his arm to comfort him. The understanding in her eyes had done something wonderful to his heart.

His carefully laid plans had flown out of his head, and he'd told her he would be over tonight.

Tonight! This was what he got for his impatience. He had to rely on his baby brother to help him secure time alone with Faith.

"Ben, I'm wondering if you could give me a hand with something this evening?"

"Sure. What do you need?"

Drawing a deep breath, Adrian forged ahead before he could change his mind. "I need someone to stay with Faith Martin's boy for an hour or so."

There was a long moment of silence, then Ben crossed his arms. "Why?"

"Because…because I need to speak to Faith, alone."

Ben grinned from ear to ear. "You're going courting."

Adrian closed his eyes. This had been another bad idea. What was wrong with him today? "I never said that."

"You don't have to say anything. It's written all over your face. The whole family has been wondering when you'd finally wise up. Wait until I tell *Mamm* she was right about you two."

"Please, don't. Not until I know how Faith feels."

Ben stepped forward and laid a hand on Adrian's shoulder. "She'd be a fool to turn you down and I don't think Faith Martin is anyone's fool."

"I pray you are right."

"Let me wash off this grease and then we can go. I won't keep you waiting to see your lady love." Ben walked away, chuckling to himself.

Adrian blew out a deep sigh of frustration. This was to be his punishment for involving his baby brother. Ben was never going to let him live this down, and he was never going to keep it a secret.

Twenty minutes later, the two men were driving toward Faith's house with Ben at the reins. Adrian's stomach churned with butterflies now that he was actually on his way. He rubbed his sweaty palms on his pant legs and tried to figure out what he was going to say.

Ben slipped his arm around Adrian's shoulder and gave him a brotherly hug. "Relax. She isn't going to bite your head off and I doubt she spits like an alpaca. You should drive her over toward the Stultz place and take the left fork just past their barn. The road winds up in a pretty little meadow beside Croft Creek."

"Where the old stone bridge has fallen down?"

Ben shot him a surprised look. "You know the place?"

"You don't think you're the first fellow to take a girl out there for a picnic, do you? *Dat* took *Mamm* there when he was courting her."

"No kidding? Our folks?" Ben looked as if he'd bitten a lemon.

It was Adrian's turn to laugh. "Love finds all sorts of people, little *bruder*. Every papa and granddad you see was once a young man with stealing a kiss on his mind."

"I reckon you're right." Ben pulled the horse to a stop in front of Faith's gate.

She and Kyle were both outside. Faith sat at her spinning wheel on the porch. Kyle was playing on the swing Adrian had built for him. The moment Kyle caught sight of them, he jumped out of the swing and ran toward them.

"Howdy, Adrian. Howdy, Ben. What are you doing here?" He slowed to a walk when he drew near the horse.

Ben hopped out of the buggy. "I've come to see your alpaca herd up close."

"I'll show them to you. We've got a new cria. His name is Shadow and he belongs to me. Adrian gave me a baseball glove. Want to see it?"

"Sure. Maybe we can play some catch after we're done seeing your critters."

"Cool beans."

Ben gave Adrian a wave and walked toward the barn with the boy dancing beside him.

Adrian sat in the buggy as Faith came down the steps toward him. She looked so pretty this evening in a dark purple dress with an apron of the same color over it. His butterflies returned in full force. He nodded toward her. "Evening, Faith."

She paused behind her gate. "Hello again."

"It's a right nice evening, isn't it?" He tried not to fidget.

"Very nice."

"I was wondering if you might like to take a buggy ride?"

She glanced toward the barn. "I'm sure Kyle would enjoy that."

"Ben is going to stay here with Kyle until we get back."

"Oh." Her eyes widened.

Adrian held out his hand. "It will be just the two of us."

Faith hesitated. She wanted to go with him, but what was she getting herself into? This wasn't going to be a farming discussion. She had sense enough to know that. Could he really want to be alone with her because he was ready to open his heart to another woman? To her?

Was she ready for another relationship?

There was only one way to find out. She pushed open the gate and took his hand to climb in his buggy.

When she was settled beside him, he clicked his tongue and slapped the reins to set Wilbur in motion.

At the highway, he turned south toward his farm but passed by his lane without stopping. She asked, "Where are we going?"

"Some place we can talk without being interrupted."

He turned off at the first dirt road to the Stultz place and then took the left fork just past their big white barn. The little-used road wound around the side of a hill and came out into a small meadow. A white-tailed doe grazing near the trees along the creek threw up her head and then bounded away in alarm.

Adrian drew his horse to a stop. "Will it bother you to walk a little way?"

"I'll be fine."

"It isn't far." He got out and helped her down. As his strong hands grasped her waist, she realized she didn't fear his touch. It didn't matter how strong Adrian was. He was always gentle.

Together, they walked side by side into the forest and down a faint path. She could hear the sound of the water splashing over rocks. The smell of damp earth and leaves mingled with the scent of pine needles crushed underfoot. A few yards later, they came to the remnants of an old stone bridge, an arch broken in the middle and covered by leafy vines. Just below it, a wide flat slab of stone jutted out over the creek. A single boulder made a perfect seat in the center of it.

"How pretty it is in here." Faith sat on the moss-covered stone. The coolness of the forest and the rushing water brought a welcome relief from the summer heat and the heat in her cheeks.

Adrian took a seat beside her. "This was one of my wife's favorite places."

There it was, the reminder that he still loved his wife. Faith's heart sank. She looked down at her hands clasped together in her lap. How foolish she'd been to think there could be something between them. "I can see why she liked it."

Adrian said, "I'm sorry. I didn't bring you here to talk about Lovina."

"I understand if you feel the need to talk about her. You must miss her very much." If nothing else, Faith could lend a sympathetic ear. If that eased his pain even a little, then she would be glad.

"I did miss her deeply for a very long time, but lately I haven't been thinking about her as much."

"Why is that?"

"Because I've been thinking about you."

Faith raised her face to look at him. "Me?"

"You have no idea what kind of effect you have on me, do you? You and your creatures upset my solitude, played havoc with my work, forced me to take a look at the way I...wasn't living. Until you came, I was only biding my time until I died, and I didn't even know it."

"I'm sorry." She didn't understand what he was trying to say.

He smiled at her. "Don't be sorry. Don't ever be sorry, Faith Martin."

He reached out and cupped her face in his hands. "You and Kyle have brought joy to me when I never expected to have it again. I will never be able to thank God enough for bringing you here."

Before she could say anything, he bent his head and kissed her.

Startled, Faith pulled away. Adrian's hands still cupped her face. He stared into her eyes, waiting.

Waiting for her to say yes or no.

Oh, she wanted to say yes. She closed her eyes and leaned into his touch. Softly, his mouth covered hers again.

The sound of the rushing water faded away as Faith tentatively explored the texture of his lips against hers. Firm but gentle, warm and tender, his touch stirred her soul and sent the blood rushing through her veins. She had never been kissed like this. She didn't know it was possible for her heart to expand with such love and not burst.

When Adrian drew away, she kept her eyes closed, afraid she would see disappointment or regret on his face.

"Faith, look at me," he said softly.

"Nee."

"Why not?"

Old insecurities came rushing back to choke down her happiness. "You will say you're sorry. That this was a mistake."

"It was not a mistake. I will kiss you again if you need me to prove it."

Her eyes popped open. She couldn't believe this was happening.

He sat back. "I'm rushing you. That wasn't what I had in mind when I brought you here."

"Why did you bring me here?"

"To tell you that I care about you and about Kyle. To discover if you care about me. I know this is too soon, we've only known each other a short time. I know you have much on your mind and you are worried about Kyle's adoption, I know you have said you'd never marry again, but—is there a chance you could look with favor on me and allow me to court you?"

"Adrian, I don't know what to say."

"If you'd but nod, I'd take that as a *goot* sign."

She smiled at his teasing, even though she saw the seriousness in his eyes. How was it possible to feel so happy?

"*Ja,* Adrian Lapp, you may court me, but I warn you, I'm no prize."

"I will be the judge of that."

The word "judge" brought her back to earth with a thump. Would the adoption proceeding be put on hold if Miss Watkins or the agency learned of this? Would Adrian be subjected to the same scrutiny she had endured? It could take months. Now that the hearing was finally drawing near, she couldn't face another delay.

"Adrian, this must remain just between us until after Kyle's adoption is final."

"Why? Surely it could not hurt your case for the *Englisch* to know I stand ready to serve as Kyle's father."

She grasped his arm. "Perhaps not, but I can't take that chance. We must be friends until then and nothing more."

He covered her hand with his large warm one. "I will always be your friend. Do not look so worried, Faith. It is all in God's hands."

He was right. She relaxed and nodded. "I have faith in His grace. It will be fine."

* * *

Faith tried to retain her positive attitude as the week slowly rolled by. Miss Watkins' coming visit would be the last one before the official adoption hearing. Her recommendations would weigh heavily with the judge.

After supper on Thursday evening, Faith cleared the table and then sat down beside Kyle. He was coloring a page for his homework assignment. She said, "I have something important to talk about."

"What is it?" He exchanged a red crayon for a green one and began to work on the grass in his picture.

"Miss Watkins is coming tomorrow."

His small browed furrowed. "Why does she keep coming back?"

"Because she wants to make sure you have a safe place to live."

"I want to live here."

She planted a kiss on his brow. "I want you to live here, too. I love you."

He kept his mouth closed. He wasn't ready to say those words to her. Would he ever be? She went on as if nothing were wrong. "I want you to promise me that you'll stay close to the house tomorrow while Miss Watkins is here."

"Why?"

"We don't want her to think you don't like it here. That you'd rather live someplace else, do we?"

Confusion deepened his scowl. "I don't like it here a whole bunch."

Faith drew back in surprise. "You don't? I thought you were happy here. Is it school? Do you dislike your teacher, or is someone bullying you there?"

"School is okay. I don't want to talk about it." He gathered his paper and crayons and ran out of the room.

Faith stared after him in shock. Was she doing the wrong

thing trying to raise him as Amish? Would he be happier in a home with *Englisch* parents? What should she do?

If only Adrian were here. She looked out the window toward his farm. What advice would he give? She hadn't seen him since he'd asked permission to court her. She wanted to believe it was God's plan for them to have a future together, but she was afraid to hope for such happiness.

It seemed as if she'd spent her entire life being afraid.

That night she went to bed but sleep proved elusive. She tossed and turned beneath the covers and prayed that she was doing the right thing.

When the morning finally came, she made breakfast and went out to do the chores. When she called Kyle down, her heart ached for him. His eyes were puffy, and he looked as if he hadn't slept any better than she had.

"Kyle, we should talk about what's bothering you."

"Nothing's bothering me. Can I have jelly on my toast?"

She set a jar of peach preserves on the table and waited until he helped himself. "Kyle, do you want to live somewhere else?"

He put down his toast without tasting it. "No."

"If you do, that's okay."

"Where else could I go?"

"I'm not sure, but there are a lot of people who would love to have a little boy like you."

"No, I can't go anywhere else. I have to stay and take care of Shadow. Shadow needs me. I'm his friend."

"All right. It's time to get ready for school. You'd better hurry. You don't want to be late."

She walked Kyle to the end of the lane and waited with him until the Imhoff children arrived. Faith bit her lip as she watched them walk down the road toward the school swinging their lunch coolers alongside.

When they were out of sight, she glanced toward Adrian's

farm. She wanted to talk to him, to share her burden and her fears. Biting her thumbnail, she waged an internal war. Tell him or don't tell him? Before she could decide, she caught a glimpse of him driving his grain binder into the cornfield.

He had more than enough work to do. She didn't need to add to his troubles.

She opened her heart and began to pray. "Dear Lord, please let the social worker's visit go well. Let Kyle come to love me as I love him and to be content here among Your people. Give me the strength and wisdom to guide him throughout his life."

A car whizzed by, bringing her attention back to the present. She turned and walked toward the house. There was plenty of spinning to keep her busy until Kyle came home again. Praying while she was spinning was easy, too, and she had a lot of praying to do.

It was a few minutes before four o'clock when Miss Watkins arrived for her last visit. Faith put her spinning away and went out to greet her. After exchanging pleasantries, Miss Watkins got down to business. "Have you had a chance to make out a chore list for Kyle?"

"I have." Faith produced the paper hoping she had done as Miss Watkins wanted.

After reading it, the social worker looked at Faith. "Is he to clean stalls every day?"

"It is a chore most Amish children take care of at his age without a problem. I've limited it to just Myrtle's stall. Shadow is his animal, and he must take care of her."

"All right. That's a valid point." She reviewed the rest of Faith's paper and said, "It seems like a lot of work for one boy."

"There is much work to be done around here and I can't do it all."

Caroline glanced at her watch. "I thought you said he

normally gets home from school at four o'clock. It's four-fifteen."

Faith rose to look out the window. The lane was empty. "He should be here any minute."

"I'm concerned that he doesn't have enough supervision on his way to and from school."

"Amish children walk to school. He doesn't walk alone. The Imhoff children walk with him."

The two women sat together in silence until another fifteen minutes had passed. Faith rose to her feet again as worry gnawed at her insides. She opened the door and walked out onto the porch. Had Kyle gone to Adrian's instead of coming home?

A splotch of red by the barn caught her eye. Kyle's lunch pail sat beside the barn door. She turned to Miss Watkins. "He's here. That's his lunch cooler by the barn door. He must have gone to do his chores first."

Faith walked down the steps and crossed the yard with Miss Watkins right behind her. As soon as Faith opened the door, she knew something was wrong. Myrtle was calling frantically for her baby as she rushed from one side of the stall to the other. Shadow was gone.

"Oh, Kyle. What have you done now?"

Miss Watkins came up behind Faith. "What's wrong?"

"Kyle has taken Shadow. I need to find Adrian."

Faith rushed out the back door of the barn and through the orchard to the cornfield where Adrian was working. His horses plodded along with their heads down as they pulled the large grain binder. The noise of the gasoline engine running the belt almost drowned out the clatter of the mower head as it sheered off cornstalks as thick as her wrist with ease.

He was headed toward her, but he didn't see her. His attention was focused on the binder as it dumped out bundles of cornstalks and on keeping his horses traveling in a straight line. Faith hurried toward him knowing he would help her find Kyle.

She stumbled several times as she crossed the rough ground. Where could Kyle have gone? Why had he run away again?

She was within fifty yards of Adrian when movement in the cornfield caught her eye. She crouched down to see better between the stalks. Was that Kyle hiding in the corn?

A scream erupted from Faith as she realized the danger Kyle was in. Adrian didn't see him. The deadly blades of the binder would cut through a boy as easily as it did the tough corn.

She began to run, screaming at the top of her lungs to get Adrian's attention. Screaming at Kyle to get out of the way. She had to reach him. She tried to run faster, but her weak leg gave out and she fell.

Lying in the dirt, she screamed Kyle's name as tears blurred her vision.

Please, God, let them hear me. Please save my child!

Chapter Sixteen

Adrian wiped the sweat from his brow and braced his tired body against the rail at the front of his binder. His head pounded from the constant roar of the gas engine and the exhaust fumes that drifted toward him. As much work as he'd gotten done today, he knew the hard part was still ahead of him. Gathering the bundles of corn and stacking them together was a backbreaking chore.

He kept his eyes glued to the binder reel. For some reason, it occasionally threw out a bundle that wasn't tied. He felt the tension in his reins change, and he looked toward his team. It was then he saw Faith running toward him across the stubble field.

She was shouting and waving her arms, then she fell. He didn't know what was wrong, but he knew he had to reach her quickly. He slapped the reins against his horses' rumps and urged them to a faster pace. The bundles of corn fell off the conveyor belt and broke open on the ground.

Faith waved him back. He could hear her shouts now, but he couldn't make out what she was saying. Miss Watkins was running toward him, too.

Suddenly, a black blob darted out of the cornfield directly in front of his horses. They shied, and he pulled them back into line when he realized it was Shadow. In the next instant he heard Faith yelling Kyle's name, and he saw the boy step out directly in front of him.

"God, give me strength!" Adrian hauled back on the lines to stop his horses, kicked the shutoff switch on the engine to kill it and threw the lever that stopped the mower blades. The horses reared back at his rough handling. The noise of the machine died away to silence.

He kept his eyes shut as the vision of Gideon running in front of that car played out to its horrible end.

"Not again, God. Don't let me see him die. Please, don't let me see him die."

He heard Faith's voice first. She was sobbing. He opened his eyes and blinked to focus. Kyle stood barely six inches away from the blades.

Adrian tried but couldn't catch his breath. He collapsed onto the platform with his head spinning. By this time Faith had reached Kyle. She had him in her arms, holding him close. Shadow, frightened and lost, called pitifully for his mother.

Faith carried Kyle toward Adrian. She called out, "He's fine. Praise God, he's fine."

He waved her away. He didn't have the strength to stand. "Take him home."

God had given him a chance to redeem himself. He hadn't been able to save Gideon, but Kyle was alive. "Thank you, God."

Adrian gained his feet and turned his team toward home. He couldn't work any more today. Being afraid was part of being human, but shutting himself off from others hadn't lessened the pain of his son's loss. Like a knife left in a drawer unused, the edge stayed sharp. He vividly recalled every second of that terrible day.

Living meant using all his emotions. Living his faith meant trusting God to strengthen him in times of sorrow and of joy.

He loved Faith and he loved Kyle, but was he strong enough to live each day knowing he could lose either one of them as he'd almost done today?

He wasn't sure.

Faith knocked at Adrian's door a few minutes before seven o'clock that night. She wiped away her tears as she waited for him to answer. She didn't know where to turn, so she had turned to the one constant in her life.

The door opened and Adrian stood before her, his face gray, his eyes sunken. He looked as if he'd aged ten years in one day. She probably looked worse.

His voice sounded raw when he asked, "How is he?"

She thought all her tears were done, but apparently she had more. They began to flow again. "They took him away, Adrian. The social worker thinks I can't provide a safe home for him and that his running away is proof that he's unhappy living Amish."

"Faith, I'm so sorry." He stepped out of the shadows and drew her into his arms.

"I don't know what to do," she wailed. Clinging to Adrian was like holding on to a rock in the middle of a raging river. She'd never needed anyone more than she needed him at this moment.

He led her into his kitchen and deposited her on a worn wooden chair. "Would you like some coffee?"

She missed his touch the moment he pulled away. "*Ja.* I'm sorry to come running to you with this, but I didn't know where else to go. I haven't even thanked you. Your quick reactions saved Kyle's life."

"We must thank God for little Shadow. I knew as soon as I saw him that Kyle couldn't be far away."

Adrian sat beside Faith and took her hand in his. "When I saw Kyle in danger I saw my son dying again, and I couldn't deal with that. I came home and lay on Gideon's bed. As my fright faded, I felt he was there with me. He was not. He's in a wonderful place where I can't go yet. I must remain here until God calls me. I realized my fear was part of being alive. You and Kyle have brought me back to life."

Tears choked her. Clearing her throat, Faith said, "I can't lose him, Adrian. I can't."

What she was about to say would put an end to anything between them. "If I move to town and live in an *Englisch* house with electricity and a telephone and enroll Kyle in the public school, they might let me keep him. To do that, I need money. You once told me if I couldn't manage the farm alone that you would buy it. Well, I want to sell it to you now."

The sadness in his eyes deepened. She couldn't bear to cause him pain, but if she had to choose between their happiness and Kyle, then it would be Kyle.

"Faith, do you know what you are saying? To do such things would go against the *ordnung*. It would put you outside of our faith. You would be shunned by everyone in the church. Your friends, my family. Can you really want this?"

She didn't, but what choice did she have? She was so confused and scared. "I don't know. I only know that I don't want to lose Kyle. Will you buy my farm?"

He sat back in his chair. "*Nee.* I will not. Do not turn your back on your faith at a time like this, I beg you. I did, and it was wrong. Grasp on to it, and it will become your strength. It took me long years to discover that, but I know it is true."

"You will not help me?"

"Not like this. Ask me anything, but I can not help you turn your back on God."

"You know what it is to lose a child." She couldn't believe what she was hearing. She'd been so sure she could depend on him.

"I know what it is to lose a child and I know what it is to find God."

The kettle on the stove began whistling. Faith rose to her feet. "I'm afraid I can't stay for coffee, after all. Good night, Adrian."

She had to get out of his house before she started weeping again. Tears would not fix this.

Adrian took the kettle off the stove and leaned against the counter with his mind whirling. Today, he'd finally come to realize God had already given him the strength he needed to face life's frailties and uncertainty. He'd come to believe that a single day loving Faith and Kyle was better than a lifetime of hiding from more pain.

Now, he was losing them both. Not by death, but by her choice.

He understood why, but that didn't ease his sense of betrayal or loss. Faith had made a vow before God and men to remain true to the Amish religion their ancestors had died to preserve and to live separate from the world. God commanded them that it must be so in 2 Corinthians 6:14

"Be not yoked with unbelievers. For what do righteousness and wickedness have in common? Or what fellowship can light have with darkness?"

This was a mistake Adrian could not let Faith make. He took up his hat and headed for the door. He needed wiser counsel and he prayed Bishop Zook would be able to give it.

"Good luck in there today." Samson Carter, a white-haired man with a neatly trimmed white beard turned around in the front seat of his van to smile encouragingly at Faith.

"*Danki,* sir." She gathered courage before stepping outside.

He said, "I'll wait for you here."

"I have no idea how long this will take."

"Not to worry. I brought a book to read."

Mr. Carter ran a van service in Hope Springs. The retired railroad worker earned extra income by driving his Amish neighbors when they needed to travel farther than their buggies could comfortably carry them.

Faith got out of the vehicle in front of the county courthouse in Millersburg. She had just enough money left to pay Samson when he took her home.

Her farm was on the market, but until it sold she wouldn't have the money to rent a place in town. The extra money in her bank account had gone to pay the lawyer that was meeting her here today.

She glanced up at the courthouse. Three stories tall and built of time-mellowed stone, the building was capped with an elaborate clock tower that rose another story higher. A long flight of steps led up to the main doors on the second story. Narrow arched windows looked out over the well-manicured grounds and a monument to Civil War veterans.

As Faith stared at the building, her anxiety mounted. Behind which window would Kyle's fate be decided?

She remembered Adrian's words about holding on to her faith. Could she do it if it meant losing Kyle?

She closed her eyes. "May Your will be done here today, Lord. Grant me the strength to face the outcome, whatever it may be. Pour Your wisdom into the heart and mind of the judge that he may rule wisely."

Did God listen to the prayers of someone about to turn her back on her faith? When it came time to tell the judge she would leave the Amish world in order to adopt Kyle, could she break her most sacred vow? She closed her eyes and saw Adrian pleading with her not to make that choice.

Why had God put this test before her? Hadn't she suffered enough?

It took her a few minutes to climb the steps. Once inside, a friendly security guard directed her to the correct courtroom.

Mr. Reid, her attorney, waited for her in a chair outside the courtroom door.

He rose to his feet. His smile was polite. "Are you ready for this?"

Was she? Did she have the courage to speak up for herself and for Kyle? A second later, she remembered Adrian's advice at her very first church meeting.

"If I were you, I'd go in with my head up and smile as if nothing were wrong."

It had been good advice that day. She would follow it again. Putting her shoulders back, she pasted a smile on her face and nodded. "It is in God's hands."

"Indeed it is. I will do most of the talking. You may answer any questions the judge directs at you. Have him repeat it if you don't understand."

"Will Kyle be here?"

"He won't be in the courtroom, but it's my understanding that he will be nearby."

"Will I be able to see him if the judge rules against me?"

"Let's cross that bridge if we come to it. Are you ready to go in?"

Fear closed her throat. All she could do was nod.

Mr. Reid held the door open. The room beyond was paneled from floor to ceiling in rich dark wood. At the front, the judge's bench stood on a raised platform. A large round seal was centered on the wall behind it. Flanking the seal were two flags, the United States flag and the Ohio State flag.

It wasn't until she took a step inside the room that she realized she wasn't alone. The few dark wooden benches were filled with Amish elders. Around the outside of the room, three deep, stood more Amish men and women waiting quietly, some with small children at their sides or in their arms.

Many of the faces she knew from her own church district, but there were many people who were unknown to her. Faith stood rooted to the spot. What were they all doing here? As she gazed about, one man stepped forward from the group and walked toward her.

Adrian.

Her heart turned over in her chest. Tears blurred her vision. When he said he wouldn't help she had been crushed. Why was he here now? Had these people come to denounce her?

She stiffened her spine. "Adrian, what are you doing here? Who are all these people?"

"These are your friends and your neighbors and the people you will do business with in the years to come. We are here to speak for you and for our way of life. The Amish way is a *goot* way for Kyle to grow up. He may have been *Englisch* when he came among us, but he is Amish in his heart and so are you. The judge must understand this. You do not have to face this alone, Faith. We stand with you."

In that moment, Faith could not have loved him more. He had done this for her, gathered together people to speak on her behalf. *"Danki."*

"You are welcome, *liebschen.*"

The heat of a blush crept up her neck. "How can you call me dearest when you know I was ready to turn my back on our faith?"

He took her hand. "Because I must speak what is in my heart. Listen to God, Faith, and then speak what your heart says is right."

Mr. Reid spoke in Faith's ear. "We should take our places. It's almost time to begin."

Letting go of Adrian's hand was one of the hardest things she'd ever done in her life. He gave her fingers one last squeeze and then went back to his place beside Elam Sutter and Eli Imhoff.

Her attorney led her to a small table just behind the railing that separated the judge's bench from the rest of the courtroom. Caroline Watkins sat at an identical table on the opposite side of the aisle. She nodded politely to Mr. Reid but didn't speak as she opened her briefcase and pulled out several files.

Faith sank gratefully onto the chair Mr. Reid held out for her but had no time to gather her thoughts. The bailiff at the side of the bench called out, "All rise for the Honorable Judge Randolph Harbin presiding."

A small man with silver hair entered from the door behind the bench. He wore a dark suit and a bright green striped tie.

He paused for a second to survey the packed room in surprise before stepping up and taking a seat behind the bench. He beckoned to the bailiff, and the two men shared a brief whispered conversation.

When the judge was ready, he spoke to the entire room. "This is a hearing on the petition of Faith Martin to adopt the minor child, Kyle King. Is Mrs. Martin here?"

Her attorney rose to his feet. "She is, Your Honor."

"Very good. Miss Watkins, I understand you represent the child for the State of Ohio."

She rose also. "I do, Your Honor."

"Good, then let us proceed." The judge leaned back in his chair and clasped his hands together. "Mrs. Martin, it is my understanding that you wish to adopt Kyle King and that you are his only living relative. Tell me a little bit about your circumstances and your wish to adopt Kyle."

Faith's pulse hammered like a drum in her ears. She

expected it to leap from her chest at any second. She glanced over her shoulder and saw Adrian standing with his arms crossed over his chest, just the way he had been standing the first time she'd seen him outside her door. He nodded once and lifted his thumb. He believed she could do this. She believed because he did.

She rose to her feet and faced the judge. "Your Honor, I am Kyle's aunt. His father was my only brother. I can't tell you how much Kyle reminds me of him. Every day he says something or does something, and I see my brother all over again. I loved my brother and I love his child. I love Kyle's smile and his sense of humor. I love the feel of his hand in mine when we cross the street together. I know he loves me, too. I would do anything for him."

"I see that you are Amish, as are the many people you have brought to support you."

Faith heard a voice say, "If I may speak, Your Honor?"

She turned to see Bishop Zook rise from a seat behind her.

The judge arched an eyebrow. "And you are?"

"I am Bishop Joseph Zook. Mrs. Martin did not ask us to come today. We heard that this good woman might lose custody of her nephew because she holds to our ways. We wish only the chance to say that our ways are not simple and backward as some may think."

"I am very familiar with the Amish and their ways. My grandfather was Amish but left the church. Had he not, chances are I would be a farmer or furniture maker and not a judge. You'll have your chance to speak after I've heard from everyone else. Thank you."

The bishop resumed his seat. Judge Harbin said, "Miss Watkins, you've investigated this case. I have read your report, but would you summarize your findings for the court, please?"

She looked at Faith sadly. "No matter how much I wish I could say having Kyle stay with his aunt would be in his best interest, I simply can't do it. Kyle's father left the Amish faith and chose to raise his son in the modern world. He had money put aside for his son's college education. If Kyle were to grow up with his aunt, he would only receive an eighth grade education."

The judge turned his pen end over end. "The ability of a parent to provide higher education is not a prerequisite for adoption. Are you sure you're not letting your personal feelings on the subject influence you?"

"I don't believe I am, Your Honor. My job is to do what's best for him. Kyle has had significant difficulty adjusting to an Amish home. They live without electricity, something he's never done before. He has run away at least three times that I know of. The last time put him in great danger. I feel an Amish farm environment is simply too dangerous for this young boy who has grown up without any experience around machinery and animals. Now, if Mrs. Martin would agree to move into town and enroll Kyle in the public school, I think he would be much happier. I also think it would make his adjustment to living with his aunt much easier. I would agree to a new trial period of six months if this were the case."

"I see. Mrs. Martin, would you be agreeable to such a move?"

These were the words Faith dreaded hearing. She could keep Kyle if she gave up her faith, or she could stay true to her faith and perhaps lose the child she loved.

Please, God, let this be the right decision.

She shook her head. "*Nee,* I would not. She wishes me to raise Kyle in an *Englisch* home with electricity so that he might have television and video games to play with. Yes, he is used to such things, but they do not make a home. A home is a place where a child is loved and raised to know and love God."

She studied the judge's face, but she could not tell what he was thinking. He began reading the documents before him, turning each page slowly. After a few minutes, he looked toward Bishop Zook. "Bishop, what is it that you would like to say to this court today?"

The bishop rose to his feet again. "I would ask that Adrian Lapp speak for us today."

Adrian came forward and stood beside the bishop. "I have come to know both Faith Martin and her nephew, Kyle. It is true that Kyle has had a hard time adjusting, but it is not because he can't watch television. It's because he is afraid to love his aunt. He's afraid God will take her away as He did his parents."

Miss Watkins spoke up. "Your Honor, this man is not a child psychologist."

"But I am a man who knows about loss and about the fear of losing someone if I allowed myself to love again. I lost my wife and then my son when he was only five years old. But I lost more than my family. I lost my faith. I no longer trusted God. I was afraid to love again just as Kyle is afraid. But God brought Kyle into my life to show me how wrong I've been."

Adrian turned to Faith. "I see now that loving someone is never wrong, be it for a little while or for a lifetime."

She bit her lip to keep from crying.

He faced Miss Watkins. "By taking Kyle away from Faith, you are proving him right. Don't take away the person he is afraid to love. Let him come to know God's goodness and mercy. Let him find the strength to love again."

The judge laid his papers aside and rubbed his chin. "You speak very eloquently, Mr. Lapp. I appreciate your insight. Miss Watkins, would you have the boy brought to my chambers?"

She objected. "Your Honor, the child is barely six years old. He's far too young to know what is in his best interest."

"That's true, but that's not what I'm going to ask him about. Mrs. Martin, will you and your attorney join me in my chambers? Mr. Lapp, I'd like you there, as well."

"Yes, Your Honor." Mr. Reid gathered his papers together and closed his briefcase.

The bailiff called out, "All rise."

When the judge left the room, Faith turned to look at her attorney. "Is this a good thing?"

"I'm not sure, but let's not keep him waiting." Mr. Reid held out his hand, indicating Faith should precede him.

Chapter Seventeen

Together, Faith, Adrian and her attorney entered a spacious office situated just beyond the courtroom. The same dark paneling lined the walls except where floor-to-ceiling bookcases jutted out. They held hundreds of thick books bound in dark red, green and gray.

"I'll have you three sit over there." Judge Harbin indicated a group of brown leather chairs near the windows. He then proceeded to make himself comfortable on a matching leather sofa in the middle of the room. Before it sat a low coffee table. It held an elaborate chess set with figures carved from dark and light woods.

The door to the outside hallway opened, and Miss Watkins came in holding Kyle by the hand. Faith's heart contracted with joy at the sight of Kyle's face. She longed to race across the room and snatch him up in a fierce hug. She made herself sit still. When Kyle saw her, he tore away from Miss Watkins and launched himself into Faith's arms.

Tears blurred her vision. She whispered, "I have missed you terribly."

His voice shook as he said, "I'm sorry I ran away. I won't do it again."

Adrian laid a hand on Kyle's shoulder. "You are forgiven."

Faith stroked his hair. "I'm just happy you are safe."

Miss Watkins took the child by the hand and said, "Kyle, I have someone you need to meet. This is Judge Harbin and he has a few questions for you."

Faith and Kyle reluctantly released each other. She said, "Go and talk to the judge. I'll be right here."

"Promise?" There was such pleading in his eyes that it broke Faith's heart.

"I promise," she managed to whisper past the lump in her throat."

Kyle allowed Miss Watkins to lead him away. Adrian took Faith's hand and held it between his strong, warm fingers.

The judge patted the cushion beside him. "Have a seat, young man."

Kyle glanced at Faith. She nodded to tell him it was okay. The boy climbed on the sofa and propped his hands on his thighs. Miss Watkins took a seat near Faith.

The judge leaned toward Kyle. "My name is Randolph Harbin. These people have to call me Your Honor, but you can call me Randy. Kyle, do you know what a judge is?"

He pondered a second or two, then said, "A guy who sends people to jail?"

"Some judges do send people to jail, but I'm not that kind of judge. I'm the kind of judge who decides what's best for kids like you. Do you know how to play chess?"

Kyle shook his head.

"I guess you're a little young for that. How about checkers?"

The boy's eyes lit up as he nodded quickly and pointed toward the windows. "Adrian has been teaching me."

The judge swept the chess pieces from the board and it between him and Kyle. From a drawer beneath the table, he pulled out a stack of red and white disks and offered them both to the boy. "Tell me how you know Adrian."

After choosing the red pieces, Kyle began placing them on the board. "He's our neighbor. He's helping me become Amish so the boys at school will stop teasing me."

Judge Harbin slowly laid out his pieces. "Do they tease you a lot?"

"Not as much as they first did. Anna Imhoff gets mad at them if they do."

"And who is Anna?"

"She's my friend. She doesn't make fun of me because I can't speak Pennsylvania Dutch. She says her friend, Jonathan, can't speak it either and he's a grown-up. She's giving us both lessons. I can say a few things. Do you want to hear?"

"Sure."

"*Mamm* means mother. *Dat* means dad. *Grossmammi* is grandmother. *Velkumm* is welcome."

"I'm impressed with what you've learned so far. Has your aunt been helping you?"

"Lots."

"I imagine she's a very good cook. What kind of things do you like to eat?"

"Have you ever had shoofly pie? It's the best. Aunt Faith makes it for me twice a week."

"I like mine with a tall glass of milk."

"Me, too!" Faith smiled at the amazement in Kyle's voice. She squeezed Adrian's hand.

"Do you have a pet at your aunt's house?" the judge asked.

⸻ned and folded his arms over his chest. "Yes, but ⸻t and it's not a dog. I bet you can't guess what it

⸻rse or a baby calf?"

"Nope. It's a baby alpaca. I bet you never would have guessed that."

"Never in a million years."

"A baby alpaca is called a cria. Mine is black. Aunt Faith let me name him Shadow. When we sell his fleece, I get to keep *all* the money."

"You sound as if you really love your aunt."

Kyle's shoulders slumped. He glanced from the judge to Faith, then down at his feet. In a tiny voice he said, "Not too much."

Faith pressed her fingers to her lips. Her heart ached for Kyle.

The judge moved a checker. "How much would be too much?"

"I don't know." His voice got smaller.

"You don't know or you don't want to tell me?"

"I don't want to tell you."

"Why not?"

"'Cause I don't want God to hear."

"You don't want God to hear that you love your aunt?"

Kyle held a finger to his lips. "Shh! If God thinks I love her, something bad will happen."

"What makes you say that?"

"Because I told Mommy and Daddy I loved them when they left me at school and then God took them away. God wanted them in heaven instead of with me. He's very mean."

"I'm sure it must seem that way to you, but He isn't."

"He's not?"

"No. In this job, I talk to God all the time."

"You do?"

"Absolutely. I need His help to make good decisions. Sometimes those decisions are very hard, but I believe His will guides me."

"Would you ask him to bring my parents back? I really miss them."

Faith squeezed Adrian's hand. Poor Kyle. He had suffered so much. She only wanted to hold him and make the hurt go away.

The judge shook his head. "I know you miss them, but they can't come back. They are watching over you. Right this very minute. God is watching over you, too."

"That's what Aunt Faith says."

"Kyle, God has His own way of arranging our lives. Things happen that we don't like, that frighten us and make us sad, but He loves us, just as your parents loved you. Now, since I talk to God all the time, is there anything you'd like me to tell Him?"

Kyle glanced toward Faith. She read the indecision and the longing in his eyes. He turned back to the judge. "Tell God I want to stay with Aunt Faith and not to take her away to heaven."

Judge Harbin patted Kyle's head, then said, "Miss Watkins, would you take Kyle out to the courtroom and wait for me there? Counselor, you and Mrs. Martin may return to the courtroom, too."

"Yes, Your Honor."

"What does this mean?" Faith glanced at her attorney, but he simply shrugged.

Adrian helped her to her feet. "Be brave. It is in God's hands."

When everyone was assembled in the courtroom again, Judge Harbin motioned to Kyle. "Come up here, young man."

Hesitantly, Kyle walked up and stood beside the bench. Judge Harbin picked up his gavel. "Kyle, do you know what this is?"

"A hammer."

"It's called a gavel. It's a very powerful tool. If I say, 'order in the court' and bang this gavel, everyone has to be silent."

"Cool."

"It is way cool. Today, I'm going to let you use my gavel because this is a very special day. It's a day you will always remember. Today, we are going to change your name to Kyle King Martin. Do you know why?"

"Because you are going to let my aunt adopt me?"

"That's right. And when I say it, I want you to bang that gavel so that everyone knows it's official. Are you ready?"

Kyle nodded and took the gavel in his hand. Judge Harbin looked out over the courtroom. "I do hereby grant the petition of Faith Martin to adopt the minor child, Kyle King."

Grinning from ear to ear, Kyle smacked the gavel down as hard as he could. The courtroom immediately erupted into cheers.

Late in the afternoon, Faith and Kyle got out of the van in front of her house. Samson carried Kyle's bag to the porch, congratulated Faith again and drove off. On the front steps of her home, holding Kyle's hand in hers, she raised her face to the sun and closed her eyes. Kyle was staying! Praise God for His goodness.

Kyle was hers.

The phrase echoed inside her mind in an endless refrain. She could scarcely believe it. Her prayers had been answered. She had regained her child and her faith all in one day.

When she opened her eyes, they were drawn across the fields to Adrian's farm. Much of the happiness in her heart was due to him. If Adrian had not gathered the church members together and spoken for Kyle, the day might have had a very different outcome. Love for Adrian warmed her soul.

Her thoughts were interrupted when another car came up

the drive. To her surprise, she saw it was Miss Watkins. What was she doing here?

When Kyle saw the social worker get out of her car, he threw himself against Faith, wrapping his arms around her legs. "I get to stay, right? The judge said so."

Faith quickly sought to reassure him. "You will stay forever and ever."

He looked into her eyes. "Are you sure?"

"I am."

Looking to Miss Watkins and then back to Faith, he whispered, "You promise?"

She picked him up and kissed his cheek. "I promise."

Miss Watkins came forward. "I give you my word that you can live here for as long as you want, Kyle. Just promise me you won't run away again."

"I won't. Not ever. Aunt Faith, can I go tell Shadow I'm staying?"

Faith lowered him to the ground. "Go tell all the animals."

He raced away to the barn. Faith pressed her hand to her lips to hold onto the joy that filled her to overflowing. To think she'd once wondered if she could love her brother's child as much as her own.

Miss Watkins cleared her throat. "I hope you realize that I only wanted what was best for Kyle."

"I know that."

"Would you mind if I stop in to see him from time to time? He's a remarkable young man." Tears sparkled in the depths of her eyes.

Faith grasped her hand. "You will always be welcome in our home."

"Thank you." Caroline returned to her car and drove away. When the dust settled, Faith saw Adrian walking across the field toward her.

How could one heart hold all the love she felt without bursting? It truly was one of God's miracles.

On the day they'd first met, she had wondered what it would be like to have a husband so strong and sure of his place in life. Would she have the chance to find out or had she ruined her chance at happiness by her willingness to put aside her religion?

She prayed he could forgive her.

She waited until Adrian reached her side. He took off his hat. "Faith Martin, I have something I wish to speak to you about."

He sounded so nervous. Had he to come to tell her he wanted to call off their courting? His reaction at the courthouse had given her hope that he still cared for her. She said, "I'm listening.

"You have too much work to do to get this place ready before winter. You don't even have hay put up for your animals yet and your barn needs repairs."

"That is true." A lecture on her property wasn't what she had been expecting when she'd seen him coming.

"It will take the entire fall to get things ready."

"You're right. It will."

"I have hay and I have paint."

She crossed her arms. "Is there a point to this?"

He turned his hat around and around in his hands. "Your boy needs a man to help guide him on the path of the righteous."

"I agree. Bishop Zook has offered to help in just such a fashion."

"That is *goot*. You are not alone, Faith. There are people who will willingly help you carry your burdens."

"You mean like pruning my trees and shearing my alpacas?"

"*Ja*, those things, too."

It wasn't exactly the declaration of love she longed to hear. Maybe he had changed his mind. Did he see her as fickle and weak? Mose always said she was weak. Had he been right?

"Adrian!" Kyle's excited shout made them look toward the barn. The boy came running toward them at full speed. Adrian dropped to one knee as the boy raced into his arms.

Wrapping his arms around Adrian's neck, Kyle said, "I get to stay here forever and ever."

"That's something I was hoping to talk to you about."

Kyle drew back to look him in the face. "What do you mean?"

Adrian glanced up at Faith. "I reckon I should ask both of you since you're a pair now."

"Ask us what?" Kyle demanded.

Adrian rose to his feet still holding Kyle. "I never thought I would love anyone the way I loved my son and my wife. But, Faith, I love Kyle as much as I loved my own son, and I love you as much as any man can love a woman."

Faith heart began pounding in her chest as it swelled with happiness. She couldn't speak.

Kyle said, "Are you gonna get mushy with my Aunt Faith? Ben said you were gonna."

Adrian grew serious as he gazed into Faith's eyes. "I must have a chat with my brother, but in this case he was right. Faith, will you marry me and live as my wife for all the days God gives to us?"

She choked back her tears of joy. "I will."

She took a step closer and cupped his face with her hands. "I didn't believe love like this was possible, but now I know it is. We are truly blessed."

Adrian lowered Kyle to the ground and took Faith in his arms. His kiss was everything and more than she'd dreamed it would be. After a long breathless moment, he drew back and tucked her head beneath his chin. "Thank you for saying yes. Thank you for showing me my way back to God."

Kyle wrinkled his nose. "Does this mean we're going to live at your place?"

Adrian smiled at him. "If that's all right with you?"

"I reckon it is. Guess I'd better go tell Shadow we're moving, after all." He took off and jogged toward the barn.

Adrian's eyes softened as he watched Kyle. "I can't believe I was so afraid of love and hid from it all this time."

"I was afraid, too, but you have shown me that a man can be kind even when he is upset. I learned to trust you, Adrian. That is something I was sure I would never do again. You've given me the one thing I need that no one else can give me."

"What is that?"

"Your love."

He smiled and pulled her close. "*Ja,* my heart holds all the love you will ever need."

She gazed into his eyes, happier than she could ever remember being.

He said, "I don't want to wait to marry you. I hope you weren't planning on a long courtship."

Unable to resist teasing him, she said, "I don't think we should rush into anything. It takes a long time to get to know a person well."

He nodded. "You're right. We should give ourselves two years."

"At least." She tried to keep a solemn face but failed. There was no way she could wait that long.

Pulling her close again, he whispered, "I'll be lucky to last a week. How soon can we get hitched?"

"With all the preparations I need to make…six months." When he was holding her close it sounded much too long to wait.

"My mother will help, and if I know her, she'll cut that time in half."

"If she can help arrange a wedding in three months, she is a worker with great talents."

"Then both of you should get along fine for you are one, too, my love."

When his lips closed over hers once more, Faith knew she'd found more than a home in Hope Springs. She'd found courage, a family and a love unlike anything she'd dreamed was possible.

* * * * *

Dear Reader,

I hope that you have enjoyed *The Farmer Next Door*. I can't tell you how much fun it was to research alpaca farming. Okay, I will tell you. It was a hoot! I didn't have to travel far to visit an alpaca farm. It turns out that there was one less than twenty-five miles away from my house. I would love to tell you how lost my friend and I got on the way to this farm but that would require a whole new book. Needless to say, the farmer waiting to give us the tour waited a very long time but was very gracious when we did finally arrive.

By the time we left his small operation, I wanted an alpaca of my own. I don't believe there is a cuter animal anywhere than a one-week-old baby alpaca. Their fleece is supremely soft, their eyes are large and luminous with long spiky eyelashes that a supermodel would envy, they bounce around like they have springs instead of feet and they hum to each other. Seriously, I so wanted one. Luckily for my husband, there are numerous city ordinances against owning livestock in my city or I would have smuggled one off the farm.

If you have not already met an alpaca, I hope you have the chance to do so someday. Yes, they do spit when they get upset, but their cute factor far outweighs that one little flaw. God has blessed us with such magnificent diversity, in animals as well as in people. Sometimes, it just takes my breath away.

Blessings to all,

Patricia Davids

Questions for Discussion

1. Throughout this book, Faith struggles with forgiving her deceased husband for his cruelty. It is not until she learns about his tragic childhood that she is able to let go of the hurt. Have you ever found yourself in the situation of wanting to forgive someone who is deceased? Did that decision give you peace even though you could not speak directly to the person?

2. Do you believe it is easier for the Amish to forgive others, or do you imagine that they sometimes harbor ill will toward others?

3. Adrian suffered the tragic loss of his wife and then his son. His life became mired in grief. Do you know someone unable to move past their grief? What can we offer them in the way of comfort?

4. How do we reconcile the loss of those we love by tragic circumstances with our idea of a just and loving God?

5. The Amish keep alive many skills lost to modern people such as Faith's skill at spinning. Whom do you know that is keeping alive a dying art?

6. Faith's conflict with Kyle's social worker revolves around the lack of modern conveniences in her home. The Amish do adopt from outside of their faith. Is it unfair to expect a child reared in a modern home to be raised in such a different environment?

7. The Amish believe that all that happens is God's will. When faced with an uncertain situation, how do we know if we are following God's will?

8. Have you ever met an alpaca in person? If so, what was your impression of these odd creatures?

9. Would you want to raise an animal like an alpaca? Why or why not?

10. What's the strangest animal you've seen kept as a pet?

11. What was your favorite scene in the story and why?

12. What did you learn about the Amish in reading this story that you were not aware of before?

13. Adrian and Faith each got a second chance at love. Do you believe it's possible to fall in love a second time? Why or why not?

14. Put yourself in Kyle's shoes. How would you feel if you were torn away from modern conveniences and sent to live in an Amish house? How would you cope?

15. What modern convenience would be the hardest to give up? Explain.

INSPIRATIONAL

Inspirational romances to warm your heart & soul.

TITLES AVAILABLE NEXT MONTH

Available July 26, 2011

WYOMING SWEETHEARTS
The Granger Family Ranch
Jillian Hart

THE SHERIFF'S RUNAWAY BRIDE
Rocky Mountain Heirs
Arlene James

FAMILY BY DESIGN
Rosewood, Texas
Bonnie K. Winn

FIREMAN DAD
Betsy St. Amant

ONCE UPON A COWBOY
Pamela Tracy

AT HOME IN HIS HEART
Glynna Kaye

REQUEST YOUR FREE BOOKS!

2 FREE INSPIRATIONAL NOVELS
PLUS 2
FREE
MYSTERY GIFTS

Love Inspired

YES! Please send me 2 FREE Love Inspired® novels and my 2 FREE mystery gifts (gifts are worth about $10). After receiving them, if I don't wish to receive any more books, I can return the shipping statement marked "cancel." If I don't cancel, I will receive 6 brand-new novels every month and be billed just $4.49 per book in the U.S. or $4.99 per book in Canada. That's a saving of at least 22% off the cover price. It's quite a bargain! Shipping and handling is just 50¢ per book in the U.S. and 75¢ per book in Canada.* I understand that accepting the 2 free books and gifts places me under no obligation to buy anything. I can always return a shipment and cancel at any time. Even if I never buy another book, the two free books and gifts are mine to keep forever.

105/305 IDN FEGR

Name _____ (PLEASE PRINT) _____

Address _____ Apt. # _____

City _____ State/Prov. _____ Zip/Postal Code _____

Signature (if under 18, a parent or guardian must sign)

Mail to the **Reader Service:**
IN U.S.A.: P.O. Box 1867, Buffalo, NY 14240-1867
IN CANADA: P.O. Box 609, Fort Erie, Ontario L2A 5X3

Not valid for current subscribers to Love Inspired books.

**Are you a subscriber to Love Inspired books
and want to receive the larger-print edition?
Call 1-800-873-8635 or visit www.ReaderService.com.**

* Terms and prices subject to change without notice. Prices do not include applicable taxes. Sales tax applicable in N.Y. Canadian residents will be charged applicable taxes. Offer not valid in Quebec. This offer is limited to one order per household. All orders subject to credit approval. Credit or debit balances in a customer's account(s) may be offset by any other outstanding balance owed by or to the customer. Please allow 4 to 6 weeks for delivery. Offer available while quantities last.

Your Privacy—The Reader Service is committed to protecting your privacy. Our Privacy Policy is available online at www.ReaderService.com or upon request from the Reader Service.

We make a portion of our mailing list available to reputable third parties that offer products we believe may interest you. If you prefer that we not exchange your name with third parties, or if you wish to clarify or modify your communication preferences, please visit us at www.ReaderService.com/consumerschoice or write to us at Reader Service Preference Service, P.O. Box 9062, Buffalo, NY 14269. Include your complete name and address.

LIREG11B

When Kylie Jones catches her fiancé kissing another girl moments before their wedding, she runs—smack into Deputy Sheriff Zach Clayton! Zach is very understanding to her distress, but he's only in town temporarily. Unless Kylie can lead the love-shy lawman to the wedding they've *both* always dreamed of…

The Sheriff's Runaway Bride
by Arlene James

ROCKY MOUNTAIN HEIRS

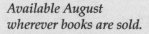